DEVIL
IN THE
DOCK

Legal thrillers by Michael Monhollon

Trial by Ambush (Robin Starling #1)

Juggling Evidence (Robing Starling #2)

Dog Law (Robin Starling #3)

Laughing Heirs (Robin Starling #4)

Devil in the Dock (Robin Starling #5)

Gone Ballistic (Robin Starling #6)

Sexual Misconduct (Robin Starling #7)

Criminal Intent

Guilty Knowledge

A Robin Starling Courtroom Mystery

Book 5

DEVIL
IN THE
DOCK

Michael Monhollon

Reflection Publishing

Abilene, Texas

For my boys, Seth and Josh

Chapter 1

"Robin, will you come out here?" Carly sounded close to tears.

"Sure." I got up from behind the desk in my office and went out into the reception area of the executive suites, where a man stood with his hands in the pockets of a navy windbreaker.

"Uh . . . a gentleman is here to see you," Carly said from behind her counter.

The man was perhaps no older than his early sixties, and, despite the lines in his face and the sagging flesh, his hair was still dark blond. His gaze moved over me appraisingly, as if he were considering a not-very-promising side of beef for purchase.

I approached him, extending my hand, but he kept his in his pockets.

"You're a stringy thing," he said, his lip curling to reveal yellow teeth so mottled with brown that they might have been rotting out of his head. "From the newspaper pictures, I thought you might be, but I couldn't tell."

I let my hand drop. As a female an inch shy of six feet, I had been called worse things than stringy. "What can I do for you?"

"Do we have to talk about it here in the open, in

front of Madam Nosey there?" He jerked his head in the direction of the reception desk, where Carly sat stiffly, blinking. She was an attractive woman in her midthirties, but she did have a large nose made more prominent by the narrowness of her face.

"She goes by Carly," I said.

"What?"

"Carly. And she has a last name, but it's not Nosey."

"Well?" he said.

I shook my head. "Come on back."

He followed me through the archway that led into the little cluster of offices where my own was located. Of the three doors, only mine and that of a detective named Rodney Burns were open. My friend Brooke Marshall, who had the middle office, was off evaluating some company's IT system.

"At least you're pleasant to walk behind," the old man muttered.

I stopped in my doorway and turned on him. "Look. I don't know who you are or what you want. I don't know what you said to Carly. But one more impolite remark, and we're done. Do you understand me?"

He eyed me. "Are you this welcoming to all your clients?"

I cocked an eyebrow at him.

"Yes, I understand you. And for what it's worth, I think you'll do."

"Do for what?"

He withdrew a hand from the pocket of his windbreaker. The hand clutched several folded sheets of paper limp with perspiration. He handed them to me. "I'm about to be arrested for murder," he said as I unfolded the papers.

The document was a search warrant for the residence of Robert Shorter, 3412 Meander Lane, Richmond, Virginia. Midway down the page, it read, "This Search Warrant is issued in relation to an offense substantially described as follows: In violation of Virginia Code 18.2-32 to wit: First or Second Degree Murder." I looked up.

"You're Robert Shorter, I take it."

"Bob Shorter. That's me."

I flipped the page to look at the search inventory, my nose wrinkling at the smell of stale cigarette smoke that rose off the document. The police had taken a denim shirt, a pair of pants, and nine kitchen knives. "Come on in." I continued into my office and remained standing behind my desk until Shorter had taken a seat in one of the two client chairs.

I sat, dropping the papers on my desk. "Tell me about the shirt and pants they took."

"They had blood on them."

"Not yours?"

"No, not my blood. I never saw the blood until the police pulled the clothes out from under my hanging clothes."

"They were on the floor?"

"On the floor between my shoes and the wall. What I think is that someone got into my house, took my clothes and got blood all over them, then brought them back and shoved them back there."

"So they were your clothes," I said.

"Yeah, they were my clothes."

"Any signs of forcible entry?"

"Not that I could tell. Cops didn't say anything about it, though I did see them looking at the lock on my back door."

"So what's your explanation?"

"I go for a walk every morning and evening. My neighbors all see me. Anyone would have had plenty of time to go in and do their mischief."

"How would they have gotten in?"

"Don't know. Though I used to keep a spare key out in my toolshed. They could have used that."

"Is it gone?"

"I didn't think to check. Wouldn't mean anything, anyhow. If it's there, maybe whoever used it put it back. Or he could have borrowed it while I was out on one of my walks anytime in the last ten years, made a copy, and put it back. Or it could be that it's not even there anymore. It's been years since I've seen it."

"You said *he*. Who do you see doing this?"

He shook his head. "Could have been a woman, any of my neighbors. They all hate me."

"Do they also hate"—I flipped to the affidavit attached to the search warrant—"William Hill?"

"Bill? Probably not. He's annoying as hell, always whining about his various health problems, both real and imagined, but I don't know that people hate him. 'Course, I don't talk to any of the neighbors much."

"How about you? Do you hate Bill Hill?"

"He's a pathetic son of a bitch, just sits and moons out the window. When the weather's nice enough, he sits on his back patio, staring across at my house. It's annoying as hell, but I don't hate him for it. Once upon a time we were pretty good friends, but we had a falling-out, a practical joke that went a little wrong. That's been years, though."

"Someone stabbed him."

"That's what the papers say."

"With your knife, do you think?"

"Could be. I can't find my paring knife, and I don't remember it among the knives the police took. Last time I remember seeing it, I left it on the counter after cutting myself up an apple. That's been a few days."

"Was it part of the same set as the knives the police took?"

"I don't know. Maybe. I think it was."

I went back with him over the timeline. Bill Hill's body had been discovered the day before, on Sunday, sometime in the late afternoon. By evening, the police were searching Bob Shorter's house.

"I'm not sure when it was the murder's supposed to have happened," Shorter said. "Not yesterday, I think. The day before, or the day before that."

"Maybe as early as Friday?"

"Yes."

"So on Friday or Saturday, someone walked into your house, maybe one of your neighbors, maybe using the key he found in your toolshed. He found your knife and some of your clothes, walked them over to Bill Hill's house . . . how far away is that, by the way?"

"Just across the street and around the corner."

"Carried your knife and clothes around the corner, stabbed Bill Hill, a man whom nobody hates, carried the bloody clothes, but evidently not the knife . . ." I paused, raising my eyebrows.

"Not the knife," Shorter confirmed.

". . . back to your house and jammed them into the back of your closet for the police to find."

"That's about the size of it."

"Tell me about this note that Bill left," I said, tapping the warrant and its accompanying affidavit.

"All I know is what it says right there. Evidently Bill scrawled my name on something before he died. From something one of the cops said, he may have written it in his own blood."

I leaned back in my chair, studying Shorter. My office was not a big one, and the smell of stale tobacco was becoming overpowering. Although he met my gaze squarely, the whole thing didn't feel right. There was something entirely too self-possessed about Bob Shorter, given that it looked as if he was about to face murder charges. Under the circumstances, I didn't like his calm demeanor, and I was pretty sure I didn't like him. "There are a lot of lawyers in Richmond," I said. "Why come to me?"

"I'm in a fix." He turned his hands so that they rested on his thighs palms up, the movement drawing my attention to the yellow-brown stains on the thumb and first two fingers of his right hand. "I'm in a fix, and I know it. It may be that nobody can get me out of it. If so, if this is my last hurrah, I might as well have a long-legged—"

I lowered my chin, looking at him steadily.

"Hell, you're not going to tell me your legs are short. Anyway, I read about you in the newspaper. It seems to me you have an unconventional way of doing things, and to my mind you've got a better chance of breaking a frame-up like this than some paunchy, middle-aged shyster who sits around on his flabby ass all day drafting documents and waiting for the police to uncover the facts he's going to have to deal with."

I didn't respond, just sat looking at him.

"Not to put too fine a point on it, I'm here because your ass ain't flabby." He bared his nicotine-stained teeth at me.

I stood. "I don't want your case. Thank you for coming in."

He stayed in his seat, tilting his head to keep his eyes on my face. "Now don't be like that. Okay, I said something I shouldn't of. I'm sorry. I can make it up to you."

"I doubt it."

He stood, too. Instead of turning to leave, he reached into his jacket's inside pocket and came out with a checkbook.

I shook my head. "You're wasting your time."

He opened the checkbook and tore out a check that had evidently been filled out in advance. He laid it on my desk, turning it so that the writing faced me, and pushed it toward me. The check had my name on it and was made out for $30,000, about twenty times what I had in the bank at the moment.

"I know I don't got what you might call a winsome personality, so I compensate. A lot of times I find a big check will make up for my failure to honor some of the social niceties." He grinned his rotting-corpse grin at me.

I picked up the check.

"That's not a retainer—it's a fee," he said. "You get to keep it regardless of how much time you put in, regardless of what results you get. How about it?"

"Don't you want to wait for an arrest? You don't even know there's a case yet."

"That's my lookout. I got some bloody clothes and a missing knife, and I don't see any other explanation for it but that somebody's framing me. I want to be ready for 'em."

"I don't know what you said to my receptionist, but if you upset her again, I'm done—and, short of a court order, I won't be returning your check. I'll keep every penny of it I can get away with."

He started to cackle, but it broke down into a smoker's cough. When he recovered, he said, "You're a ruthless bitch, aren't you? I like that. That's why I'm here."

"And of course, if this check bounces, everything's off."

We had some paperwork to fill out. When we had finished it, I walked him out and stood just inside the glass doors of the executive suites until the elevator doors on the opposite side of the hall had closed on him, cutting off his yellowed face from view.

"He's a dreadful, dreadful man," Carly said behind me. "Tell me you're not going to take his case."

I turned to put a hand on the counter. "What did he say to you?"

"It was just his manner."

"No, it wasn't. His manner didn't upset you like this."

She took a breath. "He came in asking about you. He wanted to know if you were as good as the *Times-*

Dispatch made you out to be. When I started telling him how good you were, he interrupted me with, 'Why am I asking you? You've got a year of community college under your belt, if that.'" She sniffed. "He said I wouldn't know a criminal case from a case of Bud Light. Here I am, mid to late thirties, no wedding ring, no engagement ring... 'You don't have a whole hell of a lot going on, do you?' he said. It just came out of nowhere. I didn't know how to respond. I sat there kind of stunned, and he told me that frizzing out my hair and putting on makeup with a trowel didn't . . . didn't help my looks any." The sentence ended in a squeak, and she couldn't go on. She just sat blinking her eyes and trying very hard not to cry.

"I'm sorry. If it makes you feel any better, he called me a stringy, skinny-assed bitch—or something to that effect. He did manage to work both the a-word and the b-word into the conversation."

That got a smile from her. "So you didn't take his case?"

"I'm not sure there is one. If there is, we probably won't see much of him here. He's likely to be in the Richmond city jail, verbally abusing the turnkeys and the other inmates."

The idea seemed to please her. "Maybe someone will stick a . . . a shiv into him," she said hopefully.

"Well, you're a bloodthirsty wench," I said.

"What's he done anyway?"

"What he says he hasn't done is murder a man named Bill Hill. Can I borrow your newspaper?" I tapped the counter beside it. "There might be an article about it in there."

"Someone killed Bill Hill?" she asked, pushing it toward me.

"You know him?"

"No. It just sounds like it ought to be a Quentin Tarantino movie."

"You watch Quentin Tarantino?"

"He's just so twisted. *Pulp Fiction* got me hooked. From there, it's only a short step to *Kill Bill, Volume 1.*"

"I guess it is," I said, picking up the newspaper. Carly always seemed to have a romance novel going, one of those with a picture of a shirtless, well-muscled man on the cover. As for her taste in movies, I would have thought she was more of a rom-com sort of girl.

"Don't you watch Tarantino?" she asked me.

"I saw *Pulp Fiction*," I said, and I headed back to my office.

Bill Hill was on the third page of the local section.

Richmond Man Found Dead

William Hill, 63, was found dead of a knife wound inside his Richmond home yesterday. He was pronounced dead at the scene.

"There was no evidence of forcible entry, but the back door was unlocked when police got to the house," said Richmond Police Detective Ray Hernandez.

Police are withholding further details about the crime scene.

Brooke Marshall, the pretty redhead who had the office next to mine, got back from her consulting job while I was reading. She and I were about the same age—she was thirty, and I was thirty-one. "Hey," she said.

I looked up. "Hey."

"What you reading?"

"*Kill Bill Hill, Volume 3*," I said.

She unslung her purse and took a seat. "Quentin Tarantino is coming out with a new movie?"

"No. I may be starring in this one." I turned the paper around so she could see the article.

After a moment, she said, "Not much there."

"No."

"So how are you involved?"

"An old man came by, said he was about to be arrested for the crime." I told her about Shorter's visit, including his effect on Carly.

"I'm surprised you took the case."

I slid the check across the desk to her. Her eyes widened. "Maybe not," she said.

"I'm going to present the check at his bank, see if he has sufficient funds, then I'm going to head home." I got my purse out of the bottom desk drawer.

"It's barely two o'clock," Brooke protested.

"On the way I'm going to go by Shorter's neighborhood, see if I can talk to some of the neighbors. He says they all hate him."

She looked at her watch.

"Want to come?"

11

She shook her head regretfully. "I've got to get some work done."

I gave her a lopsided smile. "Story of my life, too."

Chapter 2

So far I didn't have a client who was charged with anything, but there's nothing like $30,000 in the bank to pique a girl's interest. Shorter's house was small and white with vinyl siding, its lawn mostly dirt, the weeds just beginning to green. I stopped against the curb and got out. The March air was brisk, but I still had on my coat from my walk to the parking garage downtown.

The door of the house next door opened, and a woman came out to stand on her front stoop, her arms folded across her chest. She didn't say anything until I started across the lawn to Shorter's door.

"He ain't there."

I stopped.

"The police was waiting for him when he drove in about half an hour ago."

"They arrested him?"

She was too far away for me to be sure, but she appeared to be grinning like a maniac. I started toward her, and she watched me come.

I stopped when I got to her lawn. She was indeed grinning like a maniac.

"I'm Robin Starling," I said.

"A friend of Mr. Shorter's?"

"No."

"No," she repeated. "Bob Shorter don't got no friends."

"He does seem singularly unlikable. I just met him this afternoon."

"So what you want with him?" She was staying on her porch, arms crossed. I took a step closer.

"To talk to him. He thought the police might arrest him. I wanted to talk about why."

"Huh. Why the police might arrest him is he killed poor Mr. Hill."

"You think he did kill him?"

She sniffed. "You're a lawyer, ain't cha?"

"Well," I said vaguely. In some places, lawyers were less well regarded than politicians and sex offenders.

"You don't want to go taking Bob Shorter's case. He's guilty, just as guilty as sin. He killed poor old Bill, sure as I'm standing here."

"You are standing there," I acknowledged.

"And he killed Bill Hill."

"Why would he do that? Do you know?"

"Because he's evil. That Bob Shorter would kill a man just for the pleasure of watching him die."

"Has he ever killed a man before?"

She pressed her lips together, which I took as a no.

"What makes him evil?" I asked.

"What makes any man evil? The blackness of his soul, damn it to hell."

"What's he done, though? How has the evil manifested itself?" I was trying to sound less like a lawyer, more blue-collar. You could see how that was working out.

14

"What hasn't he done?" the woman retorted.

I waited. When she didn't say anything, I said, "You can't actually see the color of his soul."

"Oh, can't I?" She smirked with the satisfaction of having delivered the perfect refutation.

"Well, his soul doesn't have to be black, does it? It could be puke green and covered with pimples and sores. The point you're making is he's a bad man."

"Yes, he is. That's my point exactly."

"He's a bad man who's done bad things," I prompted.

"Oh, yes. Bad things."

"What's your name, anyway?" I'd been moving closer as we talked. Now I put a foot on the step leading up to her porch and held out a hand. She didn't take it—her arms remained folded across her chest—but she did tell me her name.

"Jenn. Jenn Entwistle."

"Glad to meet you, Jenn. You know about some of these bad things he's done. I don't, but I'd like to."

She raised her eyebrows. "And how long you say you known him?"

"A couple of hours. He did make my receptionist cry, but that's all I know about so far."

"You know he killed Bill Hill."

"Well, no. What I know is that the police have charged him with killing Bill Hill."

"And why would they charge him if he ain't done it?" Her tone was richly patronizing. "You tell me that, Ms. Lawyer."

"Because there's evidence that points to him," I suggested.

"Exactly."

"But maybe there's another explanation for the evidence that seems to point to him."

"What kind of explanation?"

"I don't know. I haven't seen the evidence yet."

"Yet? You gonna to take his case, then?"

"I guess I already have."

"You gonna to help that monster get away with murder."

"No, I hope not. If he committed murder, I wouldn't want him to get away with it." My expression was as mild as I could make it as I met her glare.

"So what you gonna do?"

"Examine the evidence to see if there might be an innocent explanation. Make the prosecution prove its case."

She blew me a raspberry. "Ain't nothing innocent about Bob Shorter."

"Probably not."

"So why're you helping him?"

"I don't like him. He may be a monster just like you say he is, but there are a lot of monsters out there. All of them can't have killed Bill Hill."

"I can't believe it. You're unbelievable."

"He's entitled to his day in court like any of us would be."

"You're a monster yourself, ain't ya? All you lawyers."

I tried a smile on her. "I like to think not."

She lifted her chin. "I don't have nothing more to say to you." She turned and jerked open her door. After she went in, she slammed it behind her. So much for the power of a smile.

Bill Hill had lived around the corner in a split-level house that probably dated from the 1950s. It was part brick, but the eaves and the second-floor siding were badly in need of a good paint job. I let myself into the backyard through the gate in a wobbly chain-link fence. Bill had a small patio outside his back door, a square of cement with a single lawn chair sitting on it, one of the chair's crisscrossing straps broken and hanging down. The yard in back was like the front, with more clover and henbit than fescue. Against the house to one side of the patio was a big, rust-spotted tank for heating oil.

The back door, though it may not have been locked when the police came, was locked now. Peering through the glass, I could see a bit of the kitchen with a small table against one wall and two chairs. I hoped he had occasionally had a visitor to occupy one of them. I checked under the fraying rope doormat for a house key, then on the sill of the nearest window. No luck. If I wanted to take a look through Hill's house, I was going to have to be more creative.

The fabric of the lawn chair stretched and popped as I took a seat to consider my options. Neither Bill nor his neighbors had a privacy fence, and the backyards were separated only by waist-high chain-link fences. The house next door to Bill's was on the corner, and I could see directly across its backyard to the front of Shorter's house. Bill's chair faced Shorter's house, in fact, as if to allow him to watch Shorter come and go on his twice-daily walks. It was not a prosperous neighborhood, but I liked its openness. People could know their neighbors here. They could have a sense of community.

A curtain moved in a window of the house next door. I watched it out of the corner of my eye, but it didn't move again. Judging by the size and placement of the window, I thought it might be the window over the kitchen sink.

I got up and went back around Hill's house, letting myself through the gate again. There were a few scraggly bushes along the house's foundation, looking as forlorn and neglected as the house itself. Just to be thorough, I tried the front door, but it was locked tight.

Next door to Bill's, where I'd seen the curtain move, I stepped up onto the front stoop and rang the bell. Chimes sounded, but no one came to the door.

"Hello?" I said.

Silence.

"My name is Robin Starling. Your neighbor Jenn suggested I might talk to you." Okay, so Jenn had done nothing of the sort. Desperate times call for lying like a son of a gun. "I was hoping to get some information about your neighborhood."

I had started to turn away when the dead bolt clicked back. The door opened, and the pale face of a woman with pale hair appeared in the narrow opening. She looked up at me with the anxious expression of someone who feared unpleasantness.

"Hi," I said. "Thanks for opening the door."

"Jenn didn't send you," she said in a voice so soft I had to lean in to hear her.

I dropped my gaze, doing what I could to look abashed. "Well, no. She did spend some time talking to me. I was hoping you would, too." I refrained from putting my hands behind my back and digging my toe into her welcome mat. I do have some shame.

"What do you want to talk about?" she said, again almost in a whisper.

Lowering my own voice, I said, "For starters, I understand your next-door neighbor died recently."

She shook her head in a quick, birdlike gesture. "He didn't die. He was killed."

"By a man named Bob Shorter?"

"That's what they say."

"Why would he do it? Do you have any idea?"

"Maybe for the fun of it?"

"That makes Shorter out to be pure evil. Is he really as bad as that?"

She seemed to study me.

"I've met the man, so I can readily believe he is." I smiled. "I would be interested in supporting evidence."

"Jenn said you're going to try to get him off."

Jenn had been busy. "It's more complicated than that," I said. "I'm for truth, no matter who tells it. I'm for justice, no matter who it's for or against."

"Is that a quote from someone?"

"It sounds like it, doesn't it? I'm pretty sure it's not Shakespeare, but that's about all I can tell you."

She took a breath, steeling herself. She stepped back and pulled the door wider. "Come in."

We sat in her living room in facing chairs. Her hands were clasped in her lap.

"My name is Robin Starling," I said.

"So you said."

I waited.

"Melissa," she said finally.

"Melissa . . ."

"Stimmler." Her eyes were the color of the sky.

"Melissa Stimmler. Do you know anything about what happened next door?"

She shook her head.

"Did you ever see Bob Shorter entering or leaving Bill Hill's house?" I asked. "I mean, in the last week or so."

"No. Never."

"Did you see anyone else entering or leaving?"

"Just Bill. Bill doesn't have many visitors."

"But he has had some?"

"Not recently."

I nodded. My list of alternative suspects remained a blank page. "Did Bob Shorter hate Mr. Hill, as far as you know?" I asked.

"He hates everybody."

Specifics regarding Bob Shorter were hard to come by. "Did Mr. Hill hate Bob Shorter?" I asked.

"Oh, yes."

"Do you know why?"

"Lots of reasons," she said.

"For instance . . ."

"You said it yourself."

"I did?"

"Mr. Shorter is evil. He's an evil, evil man."

"That sounds like a story." I sat back in my chair and smiled encouragingly, but she didn't say anything more on the subject of Mr. Shorter's evil nature. I tried leaning forward. "What's he done?" I whispered conspiratorially.

"He killed Bill Hill." Her blue eyes brimmed with tears. "Poor ol' Bill," she said. A tear spilled from her lower lid and slid down her cheek.

"I'm sorry," I said.

She nodded.

"May I leave you a business card? Maybe if you think of something . . ." I put it on the end table by her chair. I was at the door when she said something, and I turned back.

"Don't help him," she said. "Don't help him get away with it."

"We can't be completely sure he did it, can we?"

"I'm sure."

"How can you be? Did you see something? Hear something?"

"I'm just sure. We all are," she said.

Chapter 3

Paul Soldano's car was parked on the curb in front of my house, I noticed it as I crossed my street to the alley that led to my driveway. I parked my car in the garage and walked through the house to the front door.

Paul was sitting on the front steps with my dog, a chocolate Labrador retriever. As I pulled the door open, Deeks spun out from under Paul's arm so fast that he nearly turned himself inside out. Paul got up more slowly. He was shorter than I was and more squarely built. Okay, he was chubby, a teddy bear of a man who I think would have been content to have me drag him around by one arm everywhere I went.

"Back from your trip early?" I said, stepping onto the front porch and scratching the top of Deeks's head. Paul was a bank examiner, and he was on the road more weeks than not, visiting banks in Hampton Roads or Fredericksburg or even Grundy, a little town of one thousand or so in the southwest corner of the state.

"I didn't go anywhere. I'm in town this week, remember?"

I hadn't remembered. Feeling a pang of guilt for not keeping better track of him, I kissed him on the mouth. Deeks head-butted my thigh to regain my attention, and I broke the kiss just as Paul seemed to be getting into it.

"I thought I'd surprise you," he said, giving Deeks a look as Deeks stuck his nose between my legs just above my knees for some serious head scratching.

"With dinner? You brought food?" Deeks's tail was going ninety-to-nothing as I scratched. I bent over him to rub his sides.

"Well, no," Paul said. "The surprise is that you have a dinner guest—me. I thought you might have the food."

I looked up at him, still scratching Deeks. "Salad, some deli meat, a balsamic vinaigrette," I said.

"And beer. Remember? I brought over that case of Löwenbräu."

"Very considerate." I myself didn't drink beer, but it did give me something to offer my teddy-bear boyfriend when he came over. I straightened. "Well, come in. It's getting chilly out here. I thought you knew where my spare key was."

"I do know where your spare key is. In fact, I let myself in before I went over to get Deacon."

When I was at work, my dog stayed across the street with a retired physician named Dr. McDermott. I liked to think it gave them both some welcome companionship. "I can see you got Deacon," I said. "Why didn't the two of you go in?"

"He wouldn't let me go in."

I stopped with my hand on the doorknob. "What do you mean, he wouldn't let you go in?"

"Actually, it would be more accurate to say he wouldn't let me stay in. I went over and visited with

Dr. McDermott, and when I left Deacon was perfectly happy to go with me. He ran here and there as we crossed the street, kept circling back to give my hand a lick—it was like I was his best friend. I opened the door to your house, and he bounded past me, streaked into the kitchen and then back into the bedroom looking for you. I was still in the entrance hall when he realized you weren't home and came back to eject me from the house."

"He's a dog. How did he eject you?"

"He growled at me."

"Ooh. He growled at you."

"I'm serious. He came toward me with his head down and his tail down, a big rumble deep in his throat. I tried to walk past him, and he lunged at me."

"Lunged at you? Deeks?"

"And he was snarling. I took a step back, and he took a step forward. I talked to him, called him by name, tried to walk past him again, but it was a no go. Finally, I just went back outside to wait for you. Deacon came with me, and as soon as the door closed behind us, it was like a switch flipped. He was my best friend again."

I bent over Deeks to hold his head and look him in the face. "What's the matter with you?" I asked him. "You know Paul is our friend."

Paul said, "We're buddies. He likes me. But he knows I'm not supposed to be in this house when you're not home."

"Let's see if he'll let you in now."

I pushed open the door, and, as Paul started through it, Deeks shot between him and the door frame, almost knocking him off balance. When Deeks turned, though, his tail was wagging.

"I think you're making it all up," I said.

"I thought he was supposed to wait to go through the door last," Paul said. "Remind him he's not the alpha dog, but the bottom dog in the pack."

"We're still working on it."

Deeks licked Paul's hand as I closed the door behind us.

"I can't tell you're working on it," Paul said, bending to scratch Deeks just above his tail.

"It's a subtle owner-dog thing."

"Maybe if you weren't so subtle about it, he wouldn't think he's in charge when you're not home."

As we ate, I told Paul about my new case.

"So on the plus side, you've got thirty thousand dollars in the bank," he said.

"An additional thirty thousand dollars. I had some in there already, maybe fifteen hundred dollars or so."

"I stand corrected. On the minus side, you're representing a man who seems to be the devil incarnate."

"According to his neighbors."

"All his neighbors, evidently."

"Yeah, it gives me a bad feeling. If I had it to do over, I might just shove his check up one of his nostrils with a sharp pencil."

Paul raised an eyebrow. "You sound more vicious than Deeks."

Deeks raised his head, and his tail thumped the floor.

"Maybe this new client of yours is a nice guy—he's just misunderstood," Paul said.

I shook my head. "He made Carly cry, or brought her close to it. And Deeks isn't vicious."

On hearing his name again, Deeks got up and came over to put his head on my thigh. His eyes rolled up to take in my face.

"Ever hopeful," I said, stroking his head.

"There's another reason to think your client's guilty," Paul said. "Why else would he pay out thirty thousand dollars before he'd even been arrested? He knows the blood on that clothing is the victim's, and there's only one way he could know that."

"He just knows it's not his blood, and if he didn't get the blood on those clothes . . ."

"He admits the clothes are his, right?"

"Well, yes."

"And you know he's a bad person. His neighbors think he's evil, and he makes receptionists cry."

I moved my head in a gesture that was not quite a nod. "Yeah," I said.

"So you've got to face the very real possibility that he's guilty as charged. Which means you're going to be working hard to keep a murderer out of prison."

"You know, as amazing as it seems, I've never been in the position of representing someone who was actually guilty."

"I think you're in it now," Paul said.

"That would be too bad. On the other hand, I'm just a lawyer. I don't have to decide if Shorter goes to prison or faces execution. I just have to present facts to the jury and put the least incriminating interpretation I can on those facts."

"You won't go down without a fight."

I shrugged. "No—but if the facts are truly incriminating, I'll lose."

"I don't know. Even if the facts are against you, you've got your courtroom skills and your grasp of legal technicalities."

"I haven't been practicing criminal law that long. I'm not that strong on legal technicalities."

"Then we're down to courtroom skills," Paul said.

There was a message from Shorter waiting for me when I got to work the next morning. "He said he's been arrested," Carly told me cheerily as she handed me the pink slip that was the record of his call. "And that it's time for you to do your thing."

"My thing is what I do." I rapped my knuckles on the counter and went back to my office to make a phone call to the DA's office. Shorter had been searched and fingerprinted and photographed the day before, but he hadn't yet been presented before a magistrate.

"He spent the night in a cell here at the courthouse. We've been holding him until you can get here."

"That'll put him in a good mood," I said. I picked my briefcase up again and the drawstring shoe bag that still held my dress pumps. On my way out, I stopped to ask Carly, "When did Shorter call? There wasn't a date or a time on the message you gave me."

"No, there wasn't. That's the best part."

"Well?"

"Three thirty-eight yesterday afternoon."

"You know he spent the night in a cell."

"Oh!" She pushed out her lips in an exaggerated frown. "That's just awful!"

"You didn't call me."

"You'd gone home. I didn't want you to feel like you had to rush over to the courthouse to bail him out."

"He didn't choose his enemies wisely when he picked on you, did he?"

"I'm a community college dropout with nothing on the ball. I can't be expected to relay a simple phone message, can I?"

I grinned at her. "You cannot," I said. "Good job."

It took me a bit under fifteen minutes to walk across downtown to the courthouse. Once I had changed out of my sneakers, which I did sitting on the courthouse steps, I went in to find Shorter.

The Richmond Police Department had a station in the basement of the courthouse. An officer pulled open the heavy door of a cell to reveal Shorter lying on a bench attached to one wall. It wasn't a long bench. Shorter lay on his back with his feet on the floor and his hands on his chest. He didn't move until the cell door had closed behind me.

"Robin Starling," he said. "So good of you to come."

"I just got your message."

"That receptionist of yours has more spine than I gave her credit for."

"Evidently," I said.

He sat up with an effort. "So what happens now?"

"They take you before a magistrate to charge you formally."

"Is that where they set bail? I'm ready to get out of this place. You know I have to bang on the door every time I need to go to the can? I don't drink a whole lot, but still. I'm an old man. My bladder's got about a one-cup capacity, and I can't hardly empty it most times."

I put my briefcase on the floor at the end of his bench. "Too much information, Shorter. You're in mixed company."

He snorted. "I'm in the company of my lawyer. If you're that sensitive, you don't have any business accepting checks for thirty thousand dollars."

"You ought to be more careful about forcing checks on thin-skinned, skinny-ass females."

His mouth spasmed in what might have been a smile, though he might have just had gas. "So, are we just going to keep trading shots in this cozy little hellhole, or do we go see this magistrate?"

"I'll let them know we're ready." I banged on the door with the palm of my hand.

The presentation went as well as could be expected, which is to say not well. When the magistrate denied bail, I protested that Shorter was a longtime resident of Richmond who owned a home and paid his taxes. "He's not a flight risk, Your Honor."

The magistrate was a thin, fiftyish woman with dark-framed glasses. I'd stood there in front of the desk in her tiny office once before. The bail she'd set on that occasion had been high, but she hadn't denied it altogether. "He faces the possibility of the death penalty," she said.

"If convicted."

"He may conclude the risk of conviction is unacceptably high. And there's the potential risk to his community. He did stab a neighbor."

"At this point, he's presumed innocent of that charge, Your Honor."

Her mouth stretched in a thin-lipped smile. "I have to consider the possibility of his guilt, Counselor—don't I? Otherwise all these presumably innocent defendants would be walking the streets."

It was her last word on the subject.

"I'll give you my findings of fact and the reasons for my decision in writing," she said. "It'll go out later today."

"I think maybe I overpaid for your legal skills," Shorter said sourly when the hearing was over and we were out in the hall.

"They often deny bail in murder cases," I told him. "But this is just the presentation. We'll get another shot at bail at the preliminary hearing."

"When's that?"

"Maybe sometime next week. I'll have to talk to the prosecutor to set a date. In the meantime, I'd like the key to your house."

"Why? I don't have anything you'd want."

"I wasn't thinking of looting the place. I thought it would be helpful to look at the scene of this supposed frame-up."

"Supposed? So you don't believe me?"

"It doesn't matter what I believe. Selling a frame-up to a jury isn't going to be easy. I'm going to have to look at the facts from every angle I can think of."

"Listen. I know I'm not a pleasant man, but that doesn't make me an idiot. If I'd killed Bill Hill and gotten blood on myself, I'd have washed my damn clothes, not left them shoved in the back of my closet for the police to find. Even if I didn't have the sense that God gave a grapefruit, I'd have tossed them in the laundry basket to wash eventually, not tucked them into my closet like they were some kind of keepsake. What's the point of that? Why would I go out of my way to preserve evidence that could convict me of murder?"

"I may be making that very argument to the jury."

"Great. I pay you thirty thousand dollars, and now I'm doing your work for you."

"You're the one who came in with a check already filled out. Do I get your keys or not?"

"You think I've got them in my pocket? I had them on me when the police arrested me, but of course they took them along with everything else. What kind of lawyer are you?"

"One who would like your permission to get your keys from the police and to enter your house."

"Sure. Of course. What difference is it going to make to me? I've got me some new accommodations until at least sometime next week."

The deputy sheriff took Shorter away, and I took a deep breath, feeling some of the tension wash out of me as I exhaled. I was going to earn Shorter's $30,000 before all this was done, maybe earn it several times over. I shook my arms and went to find out what had happened to the man's personal effects.

In addition to the expected reasoning, the magistrate's written decision included a reference to phone calls from neighbors, six of them, urging the police to keep Bob Shorter in jail because he was a threat to everyone in his community. When Shorter stalked through the neighborhood, he carried a big stick—literally, it seemed, not figuratively like Teddy Roosevelt. He made verbal threats. He had once been charged with cruelty to animals for beating a neighbor's dog; the report didn't say whose.

When I finished reading, I pushed back from my desk to think about it, one foot propped on a partially open drawer. The only neighbors mentioned by name were Jennifer Entwistle, the woman who lived next door to Shorter, and one Valerie Shaw, so the denial of bail had been based in part on anonymous calls. That didn't seem right.

I was wondering if I could do something with that at the preliminary hearing when Brooke Marshall came in and sat in one of my client chairs, using a hand to smooth back her thick, red hair. "So," she said.

"So," I agreed.

"So you can see your panties from the doorway."

I took my foot off the drawer.

"Where'd you get them?"

"What, you want to get a pair?"

"They're not your usual style. Are you afraid of getting hit by a car, or are things heating up with Paul?"

"Oh, come on. You couldn't see them that well."

"Better than you'd think."

Brooke and I had roomed together a while back. She had stayed in my spare bedroom, so her familiarity with my lingerie wasn't as strange as you might think.

"I'll be more careful."

"So how's your stone-cold killer?"

I rolled my eyes. "Everyone with a nasty disposition isn't a stone-cold killer."

"So you think he's innocent?"

"*Innocent* is a strong word. Let's say he might not have committed this specific crime."

"Why do you say that?"

My shoulder twitched in a half shrug. "He says he didn't do it."

"Ah. We have the word of a possible killer."

"He's my client. For the moment I'm suspending judgment."

"Fair enough."

"I'm going to go out to his house this afternoon, walk through it, get a feel for things. Want to come?"

She took a big breath and let it out. "I'd like to. I miss these little adventures of yours."

"Appointments all afternoon?"

"Three of them, back-to-back."

"Your consulting business is taking off." Brooke was an IT specialist who had gone into business shortly before I got fired from my job with a midsize law firm and hung out my shingle. I couldn't help but be envious of her success sometimes.

She nodded. "At some point I'm going to have to hire help."

"And then you'll need more space, and I'll lose you. I kind of have already. I hardly see you since your engagement."

She made a face.

"What? Is that not going well?"

"It's going great in the sense that Mike's a wonderful guy and he's crazy about me."

"That seems like an important sense." She didn't say anything. I asked, "Are you not so crazy about him? Is the chemistry fading?"

"No, the chemistry's there."

"What then?"

She sighed. "Why did he have to rush it? Engagement is just so . . . final."

"No, marriage is final. Engagement is a much more tentative arrangement."

"Tentative. 'Will you marry me?' 'Yes. Yes, I will.' That's a commitment. I'm committed."

"And I guess he's committed," I said.

"What? Of course he's committed."

"He asked you for a commitment, and you gave it. Where's his commitment? Did he promise to marry you?"

"He . . ." She trailed off.

"He asked you a question. You answered it. Did he go on to say, 'And I promise to marry you'?"

"I think he just kissed me."

I nodded sagely. "Isn't that the way of it? You make a promise, and the man kisses you in return."

"He did give me a ring."

We looked at it. The diamond had a squarish sort of cut and looked to be well over a carat. "He did give you a ring," I said. "And an expensive one." When I was in law school, I'd read something about the custom of giving engagement rings. "If he backs out of the wedding, you keep the ring as liquidated damages, you know."

"What kind of damages?"

"When you're engaged to someone, you're likely to engage in certain improprieties, which lessens your value on the marriage market."

Her face flushed. She was a pale-skinned redhead, and it didn't take a lot to turn her cheeks pink. "Meaning I'm damaged goods."

"No need to take it personally. A hundred years ago, if a man broke off an engagement, the woman could sue him for breach of promise and collect damages for the costs she had incurred in preparing for the wedding, emotional distress, and, possibly, her diminished marriage prospects, especially if—"

"If certain improprieties had occurred."

"Exactly. Anyway, the courts stopped allowing the lawsuits for breach of promise, and the custom of the engagement ring took its place. It provides financial security for the woman in case the man breaks it off."

"So Mike gave me this ring because he was about to sully me, and he wanted to be able to walk away without further consequences."

"It's a beautiful ring. Don't let me ruin it for you."

"Too late." She got up and left the office without looking back.

I hadn't meant to ruin it for her. Really. I'd just thought that the origins of the engagement ring made for an interesting story.

"I didn't mean to ruin anything for anybody," I said aloud, but there was no one to hear or offer absolution.

Chapter 4

Bob Shorter's house didn't look like the house of a man who could afford to write checks for $30,000. The living room had a worn area rug that was curling up at one corner. The rest of the house consisted of a small kitchen, three bedrooms, and a bathroom, all on one floor. In the master bedroom was a full-size bed and a particleboard dresser with a laminate top that was broken off at the corners.

His bedroom closet had sliding doors, both of them pushed to one side to reveal shirts and pants all mixed together on the clothes rod. I pushed the doors to the other side and found more of the same. Squatting in the closet doorway, I pushed at the hanging clothes to see the floor all the way to the back. There were two pairs of shoes and one slipper lying on its side, nothing I'd call evidence. Whatever there had been, the police had taken it with them.

The doorbell rang as I straightened, and it continued to ring as I went down the short hall to the living room. The three diamond-shaped windows in the door were covered with aluminum foil, so the only ways to see who was there were to peel it back or open the door.

Jenn stood on the front stoop, her lank brown hair lying on the shoulders of an orange top that was a size too small. "I knew it was you," she said. "I recognized that Volkswagen of yours."

"Guilty as charged," I said. "I am indeed me."

Her upper lip rose, showing her teeth. "You think you're funny, don't you?"

"Not very. Do you think you're Jennifer Entwistle?"

"How would you know my name?" she said, narrowing her eyes.

"You gave it to me yourself the first time we met. Also, I saw it on some papers recently. Your phone calls worked, by the way. The magistrate denied bail, which is why Shorter's still in jail."

Her nostrils flared. "Hallelujah," she said. "Hallelujah."

I waited. "Would you like to come in? I haven't inventoried the kitchen yet, but I can probably offer you a glass of water."

"Why would you want to do that?"

I shrugged. "Social lubricant? We could sit here in the living room with our waters and talk a bit." I gestured at the furniture—a sofa and matching love seat, both upholstered in a garish pattern, and a large, well-worn recliner. At the end of the room, a twenty-five-inch console TV stood like a museum piece, a bit of 1970s Americana.

"I don't have nothing to talk to you about," she said.

"And yet here you are."

"To tell you Bob Shorter is just where he needs to be, and you need to leave him there."

"It's not up to me. If the prosecution proves its case, he'll go to prison, maybe even be executed, but all that's up to a jury."

"Suppose the prosecution can't prove its case?"

"Then we don't know that prison's where Shorter needs to be."

She exhaled with a sharp sound of disgust. "That's just a bunch of lawyer double-talk."

I shrugged. Lawyer-talk was what I had. "It's been nice seeing you."

She stuck out her chin, her lips compressed, then turned without speaking and stalked back across the weeds and dirt toward her own home. When I closed the door, I noticed an ax handle leaning in the corner behind it. I picked the ax handle up, and a chill began to work its way up my arm. I dropped it back into the corner and stood rubbing my arm as I looked at it. Either the ax handle emanated evil, or I was letting my imagination run away with me. Neither would be a good thing.

Shorter's other two bedrooms were small. One had a metal desk and a battered wood filing cabinet. The other bedroom was piled so full of boxes, chairs, box springs, and other discards that I couldn't get the door all the way open. Rather than wedge myself through the narrow opening, I went back to the home office and pulled out the top drawer of the filing cabinet.

It held books: a fat tome by Thomas Hobbes, smaller books by Michel Foucault and Machiavelli. All of them were philosophers of some sort, I thought, though I'd read only *The Prince*. On the bottom of the stack was a slim paperback by Friedrich Nietzsche, *Beyond Good and Evil*. That book, in contrast to the pristine condition of the others, was well thumbed through, with a lot of underlining in red pencil and several dog-eared pages. One of the underlined sentences read:

> The lofty, independent spirituality, the will to stand alone, and even the cogent reason, are felt to be dangers, everything that elevates the individual above the herd, and is a source of fear to the neighbour, is henceforth called *evil*, the tolerant, unassuming, self-adapting, self-equalizing disposition, the *mediocrity* of desires, attains to moral distinction and honour.

It was a heck of a run-on sentence. I put the book back in the drawer, wondering about the kind of person who would write it, about the kind of person who would find it worth underlining. Of course, I'd studied literature in school and not philosophy. Maybe it was genius. Had Shorter done the underlining, I wondered, or had he bought the book used, already tattered and underlined?

I pushed in the drawer and pulled out the next one, hoping to find it full of paperbacks by Dashiell Hammett, Ross Macdonald, and Raymond Chandler, books about tough guys driven by their own relentless moral codes. No such luck. This drawer contained no books at all, just two uneven stacks of papers of differing sizes—more what you'd expect to find in a filing cabinet, except that these papers weren't standing neatly on edge inside manila folders. I pulled out a stack and sat in the canting secretarial chair to paw through it. Medical receipts, receipts for auto repairs, owner's manuals for a TV, a microwave, three washing machines, a dryer, a refrigerator . . . pretty much everything he had in the house and everything he had ever had, although I hadn't yet seen the dryer or any of the washing machines. The other stack was more of the same, but there was actually a folder in this one that contained copies of the paperwork from Shorter's purchase of the house almost thirty-five years ago—the deed, the deed of trust, the promissory note, the HUD-1 Settlement Statement, and the loan application. I wasn't a real estate lawyer, and I didn't see anything of interest. I pulled out the bottom drawer.

The only thing there was a yellow box with a black phoenix on the cover, an intertwined *S-R* on its breast. At one end of the box was a black bar with the word *Ruger* in yellow letters on it. I pulled out the drawer all the way and pried open the top. A booklet of special instructions for the SP101 double-action revolver, .22-caliber Long Rifle rimfire cartridge, was inside. Underneath the booklet was the revolver itself, anodized silver with a black handle. If Bill Hill had been shot rather than stabbed, it might be an important piece of evidence. As it was, the police had left it, and I might as well, too. I closed the box and pushed in the drawer.

A banging came from the front of the house, and the doorbell started ringing again: *ding, ding, ding, ding, ding* . . . Shorter's neighbors were really beginning to tick me off. At the door I picked up the ax handle and jerked the door open.

"What?" I said.

Jenn and another woman, a chunky woman with strawberry-blonde hair, stepped away from me; the man behind them steadied the strawberry blonde as she teetered on the edge of the stoop. The eyes of the two women were fixed on the ax handle.

"You're just like him, aren't you!" The voice of the strawberry blonde blatted out at me like an air horn with a head cold. "Just like Bob Shorter!"

I let the end of the ax handle drop to the floor. "Sorry. People pounding on the door and ringing relentlessly tend to get on my nerves."

"Where did you get that?" Jenn asked, jabbing her chin at the ax handle.

"It was propped beside the door. Here. I'll put it back." I closed the door enough to put the ax handle back in the corner, then opened it again. "Why don't you all come in?"

The two woman looked back at the man. I met his gaze. "I'm Robin Starling," I said.

"Mark Rehrer. I live over on the next street." He pointed, and I leaned out to follow his gesture to a brick Cape Cod with dormers that needed painting. Rehrer was older than the women, perhaps in his middle fifties, and his short-cropped hair was white except for a dark strip that ran back from his forehead like a reverse skunk's stripe.

"Won't you come in?" I said again.

Still they hesitated, exchanging glances.

"She did put down the ax handle," Mark said.

"And I left my broomstick in the car," I said.

None of them even smiled, but in the end they edged past me into the house. It was clear from the way they looked around that they'd never been in it before.

"Straight ahead is the kitchen," I said, playing nice and refraining from making any sudden moves. "There's a table and two or three chairs."

They passed through the doorway into the kitchen, each of them hunching his or her shoulders in turn. A bunch of brown-speckled bananas lay on the counter, and by the sink a plate and glass and fork sat on a dish towel. The table was against the wall opposite the sink and refrigerator, one chair at each end and one in the middle.

"There are three chairs," I said. "One for each of you. Have a seat." I went past them and pushed up to sit on the counter.

Nobody sat. With all of them still on their feet, the kitchen seemed very small.

I held up the bananas. "There are four bananas. We could each have one. Other than that, I'm afraid I don't have anything to offer you."

"I wouldn't eat nothing of his," Jenn said darkly.

"I don't guess I would, either," I said. I put the bananas down and waited. Still, nobody sat down. Nobody said anything.

"Is anybody going to tell me why you're here?" I asked.

Mark Rehrer cleared his throat. "You can't represent Bob Shorter. We're here to tell you that. To convince you, if we can."

"He's evil!" the strawberry blonde boomed in her hoarse voice. "I don't see how you can not know that, if you've met him."

"Why do you care? Some lawyer's going to represent him. What difference does it make whether it's me or someone else?"

The two women looked at Mark, who cleared his throat.

"We've read about you," he said. "In the paper."

"You don't never lose!" the strawberry blonde said.

"I don't think we've met," I said. "Are you Valerie Shaw?"

She looked at Jenn, who said, "I didn't tell her."

"It's not voodoo," I said. "You were one of the ones who called in claiming Bob Shorter was a danger to the community."

After a moment she said, "I knew I shouldn't have given my name."

"Sure you should've," Jenn said. "It's helped to keep him in jail where he belongs."

"Do you?" Mark asked me. "Lose?"

"I do. I'm only six for ten in civil jury trials, which is a respectable record but hardly extraordinary."

"I'm not talking civil trials," Mark said. "Have you ever lost a criminal case?"

I shook my head. "I haven't had many criminal cases. I have a perfect record so far because I'm young and inexperienced. And lucky. I have to concede there's a good bit of luck in there."

"So what are you doing here?" Jenn asked. "This is the second time you've been here to his house, and this ain't no courtroom."

"I'm looking for facts."

"Have you found any?" Mark asked.

"None so far, nothing that points to Shorter's guilt or his innocence."

"You're not going to find anything that points to his innocence," Valerie said.

"Maybe not. It's my time, and I'm choosing to spend a little of it here."

"He's a bad, bad man!" Jenn said.

"So I've heard. I'd be interested in hearing specifics."

The women looked at each other. Mark Rehrer said, "He does whatever he can to harass and intimidate us. He hates us all."

"Bill Hill?"

"Sure."

"Tell me about his relationship with Bill Hill."

"We're not here to help you."

"We're here to convince you to quit!" Valerie said.

"So convince me Shorter hated Bill Hill."

"And you'll quit?" Mark said.

My head twitched, a tiny, involuntary shrug.

"Then there's no point in talking to you, is there?" he said.

"What matters is the truth," I said. "Good or bad, exculpatory or incriminating. With the truth, we can have justice, whether that means Shorter goes free or he gets strapped to a gurney and given a lethal injection."

"We don't care about the truth if it helps Bob Shorter," Valerie said.

"Without the truth, we're all blind people striking at each other in the dark."

"Easy for you to say," Jenn said.

Actually, it wasn't. I'd been stretching for a bit of poetic imagery.

After another twenty minutes or so, it became clear they weren't going to tell me anything useful. It probably became equally clear to them that I wasn't going to drop the case. Eventually they shuffled out of the kitchen in the direction of the front door, but the women stopped dead in the living room, and Mark Rehrer stopped to keep from running into them from behind. I pushed past them and went to the door. The women were looking at the ax handle, still leaning in the corner like an evil talisman. I opened the door to hide it from view.

"I'm going to be here a little longer," I said. "Shall I expect a return visit with torches and pitchforks?"

Mark shook his head. Jenn said, "No, you've picked your side, and we can see there ain't no use trying to get you to change your mind." They went out, and I closed the door. For a while I stood looking down at the ax handle. It was a little darker near each end, perhaps where Shorter had gripped it, but it really was just an ax handle. I went back to the kitchen.

No facts occupied the refrigerator, either incriminating or exculpatory, just a tub of plain yogurt, a carton with two eggs in it, a half loaf of bread, and, in the door, a square bottle of honey bourbon. A carton of chocolate ice cream and a half-empty package of frozen peas were in the freezer compartment.

I went to the back door, where wooden steps led down to an unfenced yard of hard-packed dirt with a Caprice Classic of indeterminate color sitting not far from the bottom of the steps—Shorter's car, presumably.

Opposite the back door to the house was another door. I opened it to see wooden steps leading down into darkness. I groped for a light switch and found one, but nothing happened when I flipped it.

I started down the steps. The third one squeaked loudly, and I stopped. *Cue the spooky music,* I thought. I shifted my weight, and the step squeaked again. I took a breath and went down a few more steps. The air had a musty smell. Did Shorter ever come down here? Not much light filtered down from the kitchen, and I couldn't see a thing.

Upstairs the neighbors started on the doorbell again, *ding, ding, ding, ding, ding.* Maybe they were back with their torches and pitchforks after all. Just as I found another switch at the bottom of the steps, somebody started banging on the door. This light switch worked, and a bare bulb came on in the middle of a ceiling that had been dry-walled, but never taped and painted. I was in a basement with a concrete floor that had a drain in the middle of it. A washing machine and clothes dryer were in the corner, next to a sofa that might have been rescued from somebody's curb. That was it except for a boxer's speed bag bolted to the ceiling. My brother had had one of those things in our basement when I was growing up.

The banging and doorbell ringing stopped, and I went to the bag and hit it with the heel of my fist: *wap*, *wap*, *wap*. I looked back up the stairs, but all was quiet. I raised both hands and struck the bag with my left hand, then my right, then my left. Punch, *wap*, *wap*, *wap*, punch, *wap*, *wap*, *wap*, punch, *wap*, *wap*, *wap*. It got my heart rate up in a hurry. Had Shorter been a boxer in his younger days? What was his story?

I gave the bag a last hard punch and was about to head back upstairs when I noticed a door of painted plywood, about two feet by three feet, set high in the wall. I yanked on the handle, and the door screeched open to reveal a crawl space with a dirt floor about four feet above the floor of the basement. Just inside was a rough stack of plywood boards, variously shaped, with poles attached to them. Grabbing the poles attached to the top board, I worked it through the crawl space door. It was painted gray on both sides, with a pretty good rendition of a skull in one corner. Most of the board was covered with stenciled lettering:

Here lies Jenn
Died in her sin
This 10-foot trench
Won't hold her stench
1190

The three-quarter-inch plywood was cut in the shape of a tombstone, although one shoulder of it had been hacked away, exposing raw and splintered wood. The poles were four-foot pieces of rebar that were attached to the back of the wooden tombstone with U-bolts; bits of dirt still clung to the rebar. Assuming the tombstone had been planted in Shorter's yard last Halloween, it was more evidence of his deliberate harassment of his neighbors, if more was needed.

A tapping started somewhere overhead, sounding as if it might be coming from the back door rather than the front. At least whoever was doing it was still outside the house. I ignored the tapping and dragged out another board by its rebar stakes. It turned out to be another tombstone even larger than the first.

Old Man Rehrer
Cut his wife from ear to ear
She died, he fried
Now they're together
Side by side
1820

The tapping stopped. "Ms. Starling! Ms. Robin Starling!" The voice was muffled, but I thought it might be Valerie Shaw, which was appropriate enough given that the third board was a mock-up of another tombstone, this one directed at her.

At 48
Val had no mate
Now at last
She's met her fate
1724

Upstairs all had fallen silent. I didn't know if that was a good thing or a bad thing, but I pulled out the last board, this one cut in the shape of an arrow. Red-and-green circles had been painted along the edges like a border of lightbulbs. The lettering said only, "Insane Asylum." Whose house had it been pointed at, I wondered, and was this another Halloween decoration, or was this Shorter's version of a cheery Christmas greeting?

I propped up the tombstones and the arrow pointing the way to the insane asylum, and I used my phone to take a picture of each of them—not because I had a professional use for the pictures, but because I thought Paul would get a kick out of them. When I was done, I stacked everything back in the crawl space and shut the door.

I went up the stairs, stepping over the squeaky third step, and looked out the mullioned windows that made up the top half of the back door. Whoever had been there tapping was now gone.

I left the house through the front door, turning to lock it carefully behind me, then stood on the stoop a moment looking out over the neighborhood, at Jenn's house and Mark's, at Bill Hill's and Melissa Stimmler's. Several of the houses needed paint, and patches of weeds added bits of green to the thin March lawns. I knew where everyone lived but Valerie Shaw. I wondered if her house was one I could see from Shorter's front stoop.

I was halfway to my car, stepping flagstone to flagstone to keep my heels from sinking into the lawn, when I noticed that someone had written on my car windows with what looked like white shoe polish. "Devil's Advocate" was written on my rear windshield in tall, narrow letters, and "Mouth of

Satan" covered most of the windows on the passenger side. The neighbors seemed to have adopted Bob Shorter's method of discourse: *We killed Robin, and nobody's sobbin'* . . .

Glittering stickers with the numerals 1192 marked Shorter's mailbox. I looked over at Jenn Entwistle's mailbox and saw that her street number was 1190, which had been the date of death on her tombstone. Shorter wasn't leaving much room for doubt about the target of his gibe.

Shaking my head, I walked around to the driver's side of my car. "Evil's Whore" was scrawled on the driver-side windows, and the front windshield's message was in such fat letters that it was going to be difficult to drive. It said, "Lawyer Bitch." I scanned the nearby houses, looking for a face at any of the windows, but I didn't see anyone.

I got in my car and noticed a folded piece of copy paper under one of the windshield wipers. Evidently everything Shorter's neighbors wanted to say couldn't be fit on my car windows. I opened the door again and triggered the windshield wiper, clamping my fingers down on the paper as the wiper brought it to me. The wiper didn't smear the shoe polish, but it didn't do anything to wipe it off, either.

I sat back and unfolded the paper to read the handwritten message: "The first thing we do, let's kill all the lawyers." It was a line spoken by Dick the Butcher in Shakespeare's *Henry VI, Part 2*. Of course, I recognized it: I was an English major turned lawyer. Who on this street was able to quote Shakespeare, though?

I looked back at the paper in my hands. *The first thing we do . . .* The message had the unexpected effect of lightening my spirits. I didn't like Bob Shorter, I didn't think he was a good man, and his neighbors had begun to make me feel bad about it being my job to defend him. In *Henry VI*, Dick the Butcher had been an anarchist trying to throw England into chaos. The first step toward anarchy, he argued, was to take down England's system of justice by killing all the lawyers and judges. The message under the windshield had the paradoxical effect of reaffirming the importance of my place in the system.

Chapter 5

One downstroke of the *H* in *bitch* was directly in my line of sight. I drove home leaning to one side so I could see through the middle of the *C.* At one point, stopped at a light, I noticed a boy in the car stopped next to me staring, tugging at his mother's arm, and tapping excitedly on his window. I smiled at them both through the crossbars of the *E* in *Evil's Whore* and wiggled my fingers. The mother jerked at her son as if pulling him away from a smoking hot plate.

I got home about four o'clock. I know what you're thinking: I kept pretty good hours for a young lawyer on the make. I liked to tell myself that I was able to do it because I worked so efficiently at the office. A less hopeful explanation was that my practice was so small that I didn't have enough work to keep me busy, but I preferred the first one.

Cleaning my car windows was an activity I could do with Deeks, so I left my car in the driveway and went to get him. As I crossed the street, I felt joy bubbling up in me. It wasn't just the release of tension after my confrontational afternoon, I thought. It was Deeks's joy, infectious even in anticipation.

I rang the doorbell and almost immediately heard the scrabbling of Deeks's toenails on the tile floor of Dr. McDermott's entrance hall, then the doctor's dusty voice. "I know, boy—she's here. She's right outside. Here she is."

The door opened and Deeks's shoulder clipped my leg as he exploded past me, leaped onto the lawn, and ran at full speed toward the street. Just before he reached it, he made a tight turn without slowing, his toenails throwing up grass clippings; then he was charging me.

I stepped down onto the sidewalk, and he dropped into a sit in front of me, his sides heaving and his tongue lolling. I bent over to rub his sides, and he stood to jam his nose between my knees. "Hey, buddy," I said. "Hey . . . it's good to see you. It's good to see you, too." I rubbed his sides vigorously, then backed up a step for the more delicate work on his head and ears.

From the front porch, Dr. McDermott said, "I always think he loves me more than he could love anyone until I see him with you."

I gave Deeks a few final slaps on his side, then straightened. "I have to say this is always one of the high points of my day." Deeks pushed the side of his head against my thigh, and I scratched it with the tips of my fingers.

"I was about to have some tea. Would you like some?"

"Sure. Sounds good."

I sat at the kitchen table to give him room to work, watching Deeks trail after him, alert for any tidbit that might fall from the counter.

"I'm trying something a bit different, actually," Dr. McDermott said, taking a pitcher from the refrigerator. "I made the tea extra strong and have it steeping with sliced lemons and limes." He filled two glasses with ice and poured them two-thirds full of tea. After going back to the refrigerator, he got out a liter bottle. "Then I top off with soda water and, voilà, sparkling tea."

He handed me one of the glasses, and I took a sip. "I like it. Not bad at all."

"How about a spoonful of sugar to finish it off? I'm going to add one to mine."

A spoonful of sugar is fifteen calories, but I was about to go running with Deeks and thought I could handle it. I held out my glass.

"It's really good," I said, taking another sip.

Dr. McDermott lowered himself into the chair across from me and sat back, his hand on his beaded glass. "So," he said. "Tell me about your day."

"Oh, same old, same old." I took another sip of the tea.

"Come on. I'm here all day with nobody but Deacon to talk to. He's a great listener, but otherwise not much of a conversationalist. Are you saying you spent all day in your office drafting documents?"

"No. I don't think I drafted any documents. I was at the courthouse this morning, drove over to the East End to prowl around a client's house this afternoon." I told him about it. He frowned at each appearance of the neighbors at the doors of the house and didn't think the photos of Shorter's homemade tombstones were as funny as I did. By the time I got to my defaced car windows, his fingers were rapping the table in agitation.

"I swear, Robin, you do have a knack for ticking people off."

"And I don't understand it. I don't tick you off, do I? Deeks likes me."

"No. Maybe you're not a threat to me the way you are to other people."

"I don't mean to be a threat to anyone. I'm just out there doing my job."

"And as proud as I am of you, I sometimes wish you'd find another line of work."

I finished my tea and stood up, leaning over him to kiss his cheek and say, "Yes, Papa." I went to rinse my glass at the sink.

"You don't have to wash up."

"Somebody has to."

"That's true. That might be the best answer to my interfering suggestion that you find another line of work."

"Somebody has to do it?" I asked.

"Somebody does," he said.

I changed into gym shorts and a running bra, hung my house key around my neck, and hit the road with Deeks. People were just getting home from work. Though Deeks and I did most of our running in the dark, we had encountered most of our neighbors before, including one old grouch who called after me, "That dog's supposed to be on a leash, young lady."

"Hey, Mr. Carmichael."

He harrumphed as we went by. Deeks paused only long enough to sniff the air in his direction. No one else that evening seemed to mind that Deeks went tearing through their yards, or disappearing into their bushes, or wagging up to greet them as they got out of their cars or went out to get their mail. Some waved; some called out a greeting. One bent over Deeks and gave his side a rub.

We did a three-miler. It would be more accurate, perhaps, to say that I ran three miles and Deeks ran six or more, dashing off to check out this smell or that, then running back to check on me. Once he charged at a plump cat sitting at the end of its driveway.

"No, Deeks," I called after him, but I needn't have bothered. The cat didn't react to Deeks's charge other than to turn its head toward him and watch him come. Deeks pulled up short, not knowing what to do with a cat who wouldn't run. He looked at me, wagged his tail uncertainly, then trotted over to run beside me for a while.

"Embarrassed you, didn't he?" I said conversationally, but Deeks ignored me, and, after a minute or so, he found something else of interest to run off and investigate.

I was in the driveway washing the shoe polish off my windows when my cell phone rang. I put the hose down to fish the phone out of the pocket of my gym shorts, and Deeks lapped the water that arched from the end of it in a tiny fountain.

"Hey, Paul."

"Hey. Where are you?"

"At home."

"No, you're not."

"I'm around back in the driveway. Someone scrawled graffiti on my car windows, and I'm washing the whole car while I'm at it."

"I'm coming out," he said.

"You're inside?"

"All of us are."

"All of you?"

"Yeah. Hang on a minute."

"All of us" turned out to be Paul and Brooke and Mike. They came out through the garage, Mike saying, "We brought Italian. I thought we were going to have to eat without you."

Paul said, "We also brought two bottles of Sangiovese—Mike did." Mike McMillan, in addition to being Brooke's fiancé, was Paul's best friend and had been since high school.

"Hey," Brooke said. "This dog is wet." She pushed at Deeks, who was trying to rub his head against her leg.

"Deeks! At least he's not jumping on you."

She had both of her hands on his head now, fending him off.

"He keeps leaping in front of the hose," I said. "We've been running, so he's hot and naturally assumes I got the hose out for his benefit."

Paul kissed my cheek, which was damp with soapy water and probably salty with dried sweat, but neither seemed to bother him. "Where did you pick up the graffiti?" He peered at the windshield, moving his head to change the angle. "Lawyer Bitch? Is that what it says?"

"The worst was Evil's Whore on this side, I think. It freaked out a boy and his momma on the way home."

"That's pretty personal. I don't like it."

"I don't like it, either. Wait. 'Evil's Whore' isn't personal. What are you trying to say? What's 'Evil's Whore' got to do with me?"

"I meant Lawyer . . . you know. Whoever did this knows what you do for a living. Where did it happen?"

"Tell you about it over dinner. Here, you guys finish this, and I'll get cleaned up." I picked up the bucket, which contained soapy water and a sopping T-shirt for scrubbing, and handed it to Paul, kissing him on the mouth as I made the transfer.

"We'll get all wet," Brooke said. "We're not dressed for it."

"Deeks will help you." I went inside, feeling only a twinge of guilt at using my feminine wiles to get Paul to take over washing my car. After all, everyone wanted to eat as soon as possible.

It probably says something about the Robin-centric nature of my universe that I assumed the evening's conversation would be about me and my new case. We weren't halfway through our salads, though, before I detected tension between Brooke and Mike. It took longer than it should have, but, as I say, I was distracted by thoughts of myself and what was going on in my own life.

"So," I said to Brooke, who was sitting across from me at the kitchen table. "How was your day?"

"Fine."

She continued to chew her salad savagely, and even crispy leaves of iceberg lettuce didn't call for that. Paul gave me an infinitesimal head shake. Aside from a quick shift of his gaze in Brooke's direction, Mike didn't react.

"That good, huh?" I said.

Mike said, "You were going to tell us about the graffiti on your car windows?"

"I can do that." I gave them a brief synopsis over my chicken marsala, conscious that whatever we were not talking about was more engaging than my material. I caught Paul's gaze, but he ignored my lifted eyebrow as he finished chewing his mouthful of chicken parmesan and swallowed.

"I know you think of these neighbors of Shorter's as a bunch of harmless busybodies," he said, "but you shouldn't underestimate their capacity for violence."

"These are ordinary, middle-aged folk, and so far most of them are female."

"Females can be as vicious as they come," Paul said. Mike's eyes started to move toward Brooke, but he stopped them. "And ordinary, middle-aged folks can turn violent, too, when they're threatened," Paul continued. "You're stepping into the middle of a neighborhood feud, and you might just get caught in the cross fire."

Brooke's gaze went to Mike, and for a moment their eyes met. I'd been thinking I could wait until I had Brooke alone to get the story from her, but not knowing the cause of the trouble between them was getting to me.

"Okay, what's going on?" I said. "I know Paul knows, and either Brooke or he can tell me about it later, but why don't we get it all out in the open?"

"Get what out in the open?" Brooke said. She'd finished her salad and was using her plastic fork to move her noodles around.

"Whatever's going on between you and Mike."

Brooke looked at Mike, who put down his own fork and took a breath. He said, "An old girlfriend came by my office today to see if I could help her aunt with a Social Security disability claim. Brooke was coming over for lunch, and they kind of met in my lobby." Mike had a two-room office suite in the James Center, a block over from Brooke's and my offices.

"*Old girlfriend* doesn't quite cover it," Brooke said. She picked up her wineglass but put it down again without drinking anything. "They were engaged to be married, a little fact I didn't find out about until today."

"We weren't really engaged to be married," Mike said.

"No? You didn't ask her to marry you? And she didn't accept?"

"She accepted and told me not to tell anyone. That's not an engagement, that's a . . . whatever it was, she didn't want anyone to know about it. And two nights later, she was spending the night with an old boyfriend to make sure she was ready to say good-bye to that relationship."

"Which it turned out she was," Brooke said.

"As you can imagine," Mike said, speaking to me, "things deteriorated pretty quickly from there. Our engagement lasted about forty-five minutes. After that, what we had was not an engagement. What we had was one big, hairy mess."

"Why did you ask her to marry you if you weren't in love with her?" Brooke asked.

He hesitated. "I didn't say I wasn't in love with her," he said.

"So you were in love."

"I suppose I was."

"Suppose?"

"It was a long time ago. The feelings are gone. The interest I had in her is gone. There's no point trying to reconstruct how I felt or didn't feel."

"It's been less than two years," Brooke told me.

"What's her name?" I asked.

Mike rolled his eyes ceiling-ward.

"Sarah Fleckman," Brooke said.

"Sarah Fleckman the lawyer?"

"Oh, great," Mike said.

"You know her?" Brooke asked me.

"Not well. I've met her." She was a serious, attractive woman about my age, with thick, dark hair.

"She looks like me—don't you think?" Brooke said.

Mike said, "She looks nothing like you."

"Give me a pair of dark-framed glasses and dye my hair dark brown, and you've got Sarah Fleckman."

"No, you don't," I said.

"Thank you," Mike said.

"I told her the same thing," Paul said. "Though the big difference is that Brooke is a very pleasant person, and Sarah is a grade-A—"

"Don't say it," Mike said. "You two never liked each other. There's no point in rehashing old differences."

"You see?" Brooke asked me. "He defends her."

"Oh, for the love of—" Mike broke off.

"The love of Mike?" I said. I gave him a smile, but really, he should have let Paul call Sarah whatever he wanted to.

"He usually says the love of Pete," Paul said.

"So who is Pete, and why is Mike so fond of him? That's the big question—don't you think?" I looked at Brooke.

"You're not taking this seriously," she said.

"If they haven't seen each other in nearly two years . . ."

"Then why hasn't he told me about her?"

"Our engagement is about us," Mike said. "It seemed too early to be rehashing old relationships. It's hard even to think about them."

"You're saying you never think about her? Sarah never crosses your mind?"

"I haven't asked you about your old boyfriends," Mike said.

Brooke stood. "That's because I haven't had any," she said. There were tears on her cheeks. She tossed her mane of red hair and stalked out of the kitchen. A few seconds later, a door slammed at the back of the house.

Deeks, who had gotten to his feet when she stood, looked at me anxiously. Paul and Mike were looking at me, too, Mike with an expression almost identical to Deeks's.

"I have to say I didn't see that coming," Mike said.

"In college she told everyone she was dating a minor-league baseball player. I think it was a way of keeping guys at a distance." I'd heard the story over glasses of wine late one night when she'd been rooming with me.

"She told people she was dating a baseball player, and she wasn't?" Mike said.

"She knew a baseball player. I think they did something together once or twice. By telling people she was dating him, she could have guy friendships without all the pressure."

"That girl has boundary issues," Paul said.

"Whatever that means," I said to him, conscious of the irritation in my voice. "I'll go talk to her."

I left the kitchen, and Deeks followed me.

It took me fifteen or twenty minutes to talk Brooke off the ledge. First she was angry with Mike, then with herself. When she got over both of those, she was too embarrassed to come back to the table. By the time we rejoined the others, my chicken marsala was cold. On the plus side, I had already eaten a bit over half of it, and even cold chicken marsala is still pretty good. Brooke went back to picking at her own food, and I covered my plate with plastic wrap and put it in the refrigerator. Then, thinking a little more social lubricant was called for, I added what was left of the second bottle of Chianti to our wineglasses.

The next morning I was at my desk when Brooke came in. She sat in one of my client chairs and let her purse and her computer bag droop to the floor beside her. "Sorry," she said. "I know I behaved badly."

I waved a hand. "You were upset."

She nodded, mouth pursed.

"More upset than I would have expected from you running into one of Mike's old girlfriends. There're bound to be a few of those out there, you know."

"Not that he was engaged to, hopefully."

"What does it matter?"

"What kind of man goes around asking women to marry him?"

"One that wants to get married, maybe. I think what you really resent is that Mike proposed to you so soon."

"Well? What's wrong with dating awhile?"

"Love at first sight?"

"Yeah, you'd think that, but now we know this is just how Mike operates. He goes straight to the marriage proposal before the girl is ready for it—twice now that we know of."

"He's what, thirty-two years old? He may be at that point in his life when he's done with dating."

She took in a breath and blew it out, her gaze dropping to my desk.

"You know . . ." I let it hang there.

She raised her gaze.

"He might not be so anxious to buy the cow if he was getting a little milk on the side."

"I'll ignore the bovine metaphor," she said, "but that's really rich coming from you. And how do you know how much milk I'm giving away?"

I was suddenly embarrassed. "Mike and Paul are best friends," I said. "They talk."

"Uh-huh."

"And Paul and I talk."

She rolled her eyes.

"Besides, you evidently know something about the milk I'm giving away. It's a two-way street."

"You're giving away diddly-squat. Paul goes panting around after you just like Deeks, and what does he get for it? An occasional peck on the cheek, maybe one that hits the corner of his mouth if you're feeling generous."

That stung.

"And Paul hasn't asked you to marry him," Brooke said. "He's afraid to, actually. You know that, don't you? He thinks if he rushes you, he's going to spoil things. Well? Why can't Mike be afraid of spoiling things? What gives him so much confidence in the woman department?"

She paused, but her complaints and observations had been tossed out so indiscriminately that I didn't know where to start.

"You know I'm just following your lead," Brooke said. "You've done the sex thing, and look where it's got you."

"I'm not doing so badly. I've got friends. I've got Paul . . ."

"The ongoing mystery! You don't give him anything, and you promise him even less. Maybe if I was a six-foot goddess, I could get away with that with Mike."

I was only five eleven, if *only* is a word that belongs in front of five eleven, and Aphrodite I was not, but I let it pass. "You are getting away with it. The whole premise of this conversation is that you're getting away with it."

"I promised to marry him."

"Well, yes, but you didn't have to."

"Suppose he asked me, and I said no, and he left me? What then?" There were tears in her eyes.

"Mike wouldn't leave you," I said.

"He left Sarah, didn't he?"

"She spent the night with her old boyfriend."

"Well, at least he doesn't have to worry about that with me, now does he?" Brooke spun out of her chair and left my office, slamming the door behind her.

I sighed. *Another abrupt departure.* If she'd asked me, I would have told her to leave the door open.

Chapter 6

I didn't see a compelling need to visit Bob Shorter in the Richmond city jail, so I didn't. It might be fair to say I neglected him shamefully, even though I was working on his case. By the time the sheriff's department brought him back to the courthouse for his preliminary hearing, I was feeling guilty about my failure to visit him, so I arranged to spend a few minutes with him before the start of his hearing. It was the least I could do—which is why I did it.

"If it isn't the Wizard of Oz," Shorter said when he saw me. "I was beginning to think you were a myth. I trust you've been hard at work behind the curtain?"

"Do you want his handcuffs off or on?" the deputy sheriff asked me.

"Off," I said.

He nodded, and I waited while he unlocked them. When the deputy left the room and closed the door behind himself, Shorter took a seat at the scarred wood table. I remained standing.

"Well?" he said.

"Preliminary hearing today."

"Thanks for the news flash. You said this is when I get out of here."

I shook my head. "The judge will take another look at the question of bail. That's all I can say."

"So what have you been doing?"

"Filing discover motions and poring over what the prosecution gives me."

He made a disgusted noise, his breath puffing out through his lips. "Like that's gonna do me any good."

"I talked to your neighbors. Some of them were rather insistent I spend time with them."

"Warped bunch of busybodies. What did they want?"

"For you to fry in the electric chair. Life in prison might satisfy them. Whatever it takes for you never to return to their neighborhood."

His smile was without humor.

"It would be an understatement to say that they hate you. Why is that, do you think?"

"They like neighbors who play nice. It gives them power. A person who feels no obligation to play nice is a person they can't control."

"I found your lawn decorations for Halloween. I assume the tombstones were for Halloween."

This time his grin held a touch of humor.

"So you're not above playing games of your own," I said.

"When they amuse me."

"What's amusing about them?"

"Oh, come on. You saw the tombstones. They're hilarious. You've got to admit that."

"They're witty," I conceded. "You had to know they'd upset people."

"A little clean fun, all perfectly legal."

"Maybe."

"They pooled their money to hire a lawyer to go after me. He wrote me a couple of threatening letters. I ignored them. After that, nada."

"I might have had a go at proving libel. Maybe intentional infliction of emotional distress."

"Fortunately, they didn't hire you. The lawyer they got didn't have your cojones."

I ignored his dubious grasp of the female anatomy. "You don't have a pleasant bone in your body, do you?"

"I told you, niceness is an obligation the weak impose on the people around them in an effort to control them. Why should I play?"

"Your natural disposition to benevolence?"

"Evidently, I have no such disposition."

"And evidently, you don't consider that a failing."

"I consider it a strength," he said.

"Suppose you're wrong about that?"

"Some may find it undesirable. Who's to say it's a failing?"

"The great weight of public opinion?" I offered.

"What, majority opinion determines what's right and wrong? You see how ridiculous that is, don't you? All I have to do is convert enough people to my way of thinking, and I'll have right on my side."

"I can't see you as that persuasive." I stepped to the door and slapped my palm against it. The deputy sheriff had his hand on the butt of his gun as he pushed the door open.

"We might as well go," I told him. "We're not accomplishing anything here."

"What?" Shorter asked from behind me. "We're not going to go over my testimony?"

I turned to look at him. "To put you on the stand in a preliminary hearing, I'd have to be as bad a lawyer as you think I am."

"I haven't said you're a bad lawyer. How would I know? So far I haven't seen jack from you."

At the hearing, the prosecution introduced evidence as to cause of death—a stab wound to the chest—and the presence of bloody clothing in Shorter's closet. The blood's DNA profile matched the profile of Hill's blood, just as Shorter had suspected from the moment he saw it. I did find out something about the murder weapon, a stainless steel knife with a three-and-a-quarter-inch blade. Detective Ray Hernandez was on the witness stand when it was marked as a commonwealth exhibit and entered into evidence.

"Where was the knife found?" asked Ian Maxwell, the assistant district attorney currently in charge of the case.

"Beside the body."

"Were there fingerprints on the knife?" Maxwell asked.

"Yes, on the handle."

"But not on the blade?"

"No, not on the blade." Hernandez shook his head.

"This was a wood handle?"

"Yes. Beechwood, according to the manufacturer. It held the prints just fine."

"Whose fingerprints were they?"

Hernandez looked toward Shorter and me at the defense table. "The defendant's, Robert Shorter. They were the prints of the third, fourth, and fifth fingers of his right hand."

I leaned toward Shorter, who sat beside me at the defense table. "Any thoughts?" I said.

"It could be my knife," he said. "I told you I have a paring knife that looks like that."

When it was my turn to cross-examine, I asked Hernandez, "Were the fingerprints imprinted in the blood that was on the knife?"

"They were not."

"They were just prints consisting of the natural residues any of us might have on our fingers?"

"That's right."

"Any way to know how long they'd been on the knife?"

"No."

When he seemed disinclined to say anything further, I said, "Please elaborate."

"There are three factors that might determine how long a latent fingerprint would stay on a surface: the matrix of the print, the substrate, and the environment."

I waited. "Okay," I said finally. "Now you're just playing with me."

He grinned.

I said, "Since you seem disinclined to do it, let me elaborate, and you tell me where I've gone wrong. The matrix is the sweat or body oil that was on the fingers—"

"Or it could be some kind of contaminant," Hernandez said. "Blood, dust, wet fingernail polish . . ."

"Was there fingernail polish on this knife? Or blood or dust?"

"There was blood on the knife, but, like I said, it wasn't what held the print."

"Okay," I said. "So much for the matrix. The substrate would be the surface the print was found on, the beechwood handle."

"That's right."

"And *environment* I think I understand without further explanation. Based on the three factors you mentioned, the matrix, the substrate, and the environment, these prints could have been on the knife how long?"

Hernandez shook his head.

"You can't say?"

"I'd say the prints were made after the last time the knife went through the washer."

"Or was washed in the sink with soap and water?"

"Or after that. If you can tell me when that was, I can give you the earliest possible date for the prints."

"You've said that the defendant's prints were on the knife. Were there anybody else's?"

He hesitated. "We're not sure."

"What do you mean, you're not sure?"

"There was one smeared print."

"A print you couldn't match to any of the defendant's fingers?"

"That's right."

"Did you attempt to match it to anyone else's?"

"The decedent's."

"And?"

"There were a few points of identification between the print and the print on the decedent's left middle finger."

"How many points?"

"I think it was four or five. I'd have to look at my notes to be sure, but it wasn't many. As I said, the print was mostly smeared."

"Do you have your notes with you?"

He didn't.

"How many points of identification are required to establish a match?"

"In the United States, there's no set number. It depends on the clarity of the impression and the uniqueness of the formations."

"In the United States there's no set number? Does that mean that other countries set some minimum number of points necessary to establish a match?"

He shifted in his chair. "Yes. England, I think, requires sixteen points, Germany only twelve or so."

"Or so," I said.

"What other countries require in the way of fingerprint identification is not something that comes up very often," he said.

"Have you speculated as to how Bill Hill's fingerprint may have gotten on the handle of that knife? Could he have been trying to pull it out of his chest?"

"Well, maybe, but it wouldn't explain the fingerprint—assuming the print was his, which we haven't established."

"Quite a coincidence, isn't it, if it's not his? That the print would have four or five points of identification with one of the two people who might have handled the knife?"

"I'm not a statistician. All I can tell you is we couldn't establish a match."

"You said the decedent couldn't have made the print pulling the knife out of his chest. It wasn't still in the wound, was it? Didn't you say the knife was on the floor?"

"The decedent was wearing gloves."

"Wearing gloves."

"The blood did show an imprint of the fabric of one of the gloves on the underside of the knife handle," Hernandez volunteered.

We spent a little time working out which part of the knife handle was the underside. "Doesn't it seem strange to you that the decedent was wearing gloves?" I asked.

"No, not really. Hill didn't have his heat on, and it was cold in that house. According to the thermostat, when we found him it was sixty-two degrees in the house, and the high on March 9, the day of the murder, was only fifty-seven."

"And there was blood on the gloves, I take it. Both gloves, or only one of them?"

"Only the right. There was blood on the palm of the glove and especially the tip of the index finger. We think he used that finger to write Shorter's name on the floor, that he dipped it in the blood running out of his chest."

Way to end on a high note. When I sat back down, Shorter leaned toward me. "Even I thought that was a waste of time, and I got nothing going on."

"I'll try to be more entertaining."

He only grunted.

"Ms. Starling?" the judge said. "Are you prepared to continue, or do you need a short recess?"

I half stood. "Ready, Your Honor."

"Call your next witness," the judge said to Maxwell.

The preliminary hearing ended just before lunch the next day, and the judge bound Shorter over for trial in circuit court. I asked that the defendant be admitted to bail. As the magistrate had done before him, the judge declined. As the courtroom cleared, Shorter said, "You said I was going to see some action at the preliminary hearing."

"You did. We got an outline of the prosecution's case against you, and we got to cross-examine the two key witnesses—the police detective and the medical examiner."

"And here I go back to jail."

"You were always going back to jail. Defendants never win at the preliminary hearing."

"That's not what you said. When the magistrate denied bail, you said to wait until the preliminary hearing. I've been waiting."

"I was hoping something would come up."

"Besides, I know of at least one case you won at the preliminary hearing. I read about it in the paper."

"That was a fluke."

"Great."

"You seem to think I have an obligation to exercise skill and diligence to acquit you," I said.

"And you don't? I believe we have a contract."

"And it's your opinion that people ought to honor their contracts?"

He studied me. "If they don't want to face the consequences."

"But if I'm okay with the consequences, screwing you over would be a valid choice, wouldn't you say?"

His lips pulled back to expose the brownest teeth I'd ever seen. "Majority opinion is on my side on this one," he said.

"So for this we defer to majority opinion? The majority's opinion is binding when it comes to the moral obligations of a contract, but not when it comes to being pleasant to our neighbors?"

The deputy sheriff was standing by, the handcuffs cupped in one hand, but Shorter stayed in his seat.

"You read books, don't you?" he asked me.

"Since early childhood."

"There may be more to you than meets the eye."

"Maybe. I like to think moral principles are real, like mass and color," I said. "They don't change as the public consensus changes, and we don't get to make up our own."

"And these moral principles are grounded on what?"

I hesitated.

"You're building castles in the air with this moral edifice of yours, but you are quick on the uptake, I'll give you that." He stood, finally, and the deputy sheriff cuffed his hands behind him. Shorter didn't look upset, but his expression was calculating and not particularly pleasant. He'd given me two compliments in a row. I thought he might as readily drive a knife into me as give me a third.

The deputy led him away. As I put my papers back into my briefcase, a cold spot developed between my shoulder blades. The shiver started there and radiated outward. *I do not like Bob Shorter,* I said to myself.

Surprisingly, there aren't that many places to eat near the courthouse—a Subway up near the Coliseum, a couple of places down around the VCU Hospital. One of the best within a couple of blocks was the Richmond on Broad Café, occupying a space on East Broad Street that had once served as a drugstore. Even though it was a block out of my way, I decided to stop off for a bite to eat on my walk back to the office.

As soon as I walked through the double glass doors, I regretted my decision. Mike McMillan and Sarah Fleckman were sitting across a table from each other, him with a sandwich in front of him, her with a quiche. His back was toward me. Her gaze flicked toward me and away.

I took a breath and went to the counter to order a salad with spinach and roasted butternut squash. Brooke, I was sure, didn't know Mike was having lunch with Sarah, and it put me in an awkward position. I paid for my salad and, after a moment's hesitation, took it to a table by the front window, close enough to Mike and Sarah's table for me to pick up at least some of their conversation but still out of

Mike's line of sight. I know what you're thinking, but I was acting for his benefit. Mike was a friend. I owed it to him to learn enough to acquit him of the suspicions Brooke was going to have when she found out about this—to be honest, of the suspicions that I myself had at the sight of him and Sarah leaning across the table toward each other, talking earnestly.

As soon as I sat down, though, they stopped talking and started working on the food in front of them. Sarah's fork clinked against her plate. Mike drank his tea and ate his sandwich. I was halfway through my salad before Sarah said, "You've been ready a long time. I understand that."

She gave him time, but Mike didn't say anything. He reached for his tea.

"Like I said, I'm ready now, too," she said.

Mike drank. I couldn't see his face, but his neck seemed flushed where it was visible above his collar.

Sarah said, "I thought . . . I just wanted you to know. In case it mattered."

"It doesn't," Mike said. "I'm sorry."

"I waited too long then." She sounded as if she might start crying, but I kept my eyes on my salad, avoiding any possibility of making eye contact. "I've let the best thing that ever happened to me just slip away," she said.

"Sarah, don't."

"I know. I'm sorry." She pushed her plate with its half-eaten quiche away from her. Mike pushed the rest of his sandwich into his mouth and stood with his tea, his chair scraping back behind him.

"I'm sorry," Sarah said again, getting to her feet. A glance showed me that tears had broken free and were trailing down her cheeks. She was a beautiful woman, even with tear-reddened eyes. She bumped the corner of the table as she went around it, and she strode for the door, her head down and her small purse clutched in one hand.

Mike turned to watch her go, and his eyes focused on me.

I chewed my mouthful of salad a few more times and swallowed. "Mike McMillan," I said, as if in surprise. "Fancy seeing you here."

He glanced at the door, and I followed his gaze, but Sarah was gone. Mike took a breath and exhaled. Then he took two steps and pulled out the chair across from me. He dropped into it, leaning back with his legs out. When he didn't say anything, I put another forkful of salad in my mouth.

He cleared his throat. "Where's Paul?"

I shrugged, chewing.

"Does Brooke have you following me?"

I swallowed. "I've been in court. Bob Shorter's preliminary hearing."

"Just my luck then. How'd the hearing go?"

"Judge bound him over."

"So you lost."

"I didn't win."

One corner of his mouth rose. "Never concede defeat," he said.

"'Never say die.' It sounds more dramatic, if you're looking for a motto for me."

He sat, mouth pursed, head nodding thoughtfully. I started to take another bite of salad, then put my fork down. "I didn't hear much," I said.

"You've been ready—now she's ready. I assume the best thing that ever happened to her would be you."

His head moved equivocally. "The best and the worst."

"And now you've slipped away."

"I am marrying Brooke."

"And you stood by that."

"I did."

"Where is Brooke anyway?"

"Fredericksburg, working with a company up there."

I nodded.

"Sarah called me this morning, said she was having a personal crisis and needed to talk."

"Are her personal crises still your business?"

"No. Of course not, though maybe I wasn't as clear on that this morning. I thought maybe this crisis was something I ought to clean up."

"And it turned out not to be anything you could clean up."

He sighed, shook his head.

"You need to let her go, Mike."

"I know. I have."

I took a sip of my water.

Mike said, "I don't know why she's so insecure about this."

"Well, you are marrying someone else."

"I meant Brooke."

"I know what you meant. I have to say, it's not like her. I've never known her to be insecure or clingy. It may be a reflection of the uncertainty she has about getting married generally—the permanence of it, the loss of freedom . . ."

"She's not losing her freedom! She can do anything she wants, work late, hang out with you, take up long-distance running—"

"Listen to rap music at full volume," I continued for him. "Have MSNBC on the television whenever she's home. Keep her clean laundry piled on the sofa to fold whenever she decides to take the time . . ."

Mike was beginning to look a little panicked. "You know her better than I do," he said.

I grinned at him. "I'm kidding. But you see what I mean. There're a lot of ways a person might find a permanent roommate constricting."

"So you're telling me I've found myself yet another woman who loves me but doesn't want to marry me."

"Not at all. She said she'd marry you, didn't she? She wants to marry you. There's just a lot of uncertainty in her life at this point. Having a dark-haired beauty like Sarah Fleckman bumping around the edges of yours doesn't help."

He sighed, then nodded. "I'll do better."

"I know how I'd feel if one of Paul's old girlfriends kept turning up."

"Really?" His mouth quirked upward at the corner. "I'd think you'd either chew her up and spit her out or ignore her entirely. Besides, Paul doesn't have any old girlfriends. He's always fallen for hot women who were out of his league and worshiped them from afar. Until you."

"Ah. Probably good for me to be taken down a peg."

"I didn't mean that. You're as far out of his league as any of them. This is just the first time he's managed to develop a relationship with one of the goddesses he's fallen for."

"Oh, wow," I said. What was it with me and Aphrodite?

"I didn't mean it quite that way, either."

"You mean I'm not a goddess?"

"Just flesh and blood. Impressive as hell, but just flesh and blood."

"I can settle for impressive as hell."

"So are you going to tell Brooke about this?"

"No." I shook my head decisively. "That would be like throwing a gas can onto a fire."

Mike exhaled carefully as some of the tension eased out of him.

"But you are," I said.

Chapter 7

The Monday after Shorter was bound over for trial, I cleared my desk except for the autopsy report on Bill Hill, the police reports, and the exhibit list I'd gotten from the prosecution. On the wall I pinned the crime scene photos. I was sitting at my desk, drumming my fingers and looking at my wall of photos when Brooke stuck her head in.

"Hard at work, I see," she said.

"As usual."

Brooke came in and sat down. She said, "I thought you were going to say something about how late I was, but I stopped off at a client's."

"I'll make a note of it."

As I've mentioned before, Brooke's business seemed to grow like kudzu, while mine still lurched from case to case. I wasn't jealous of her success, but it was a continuing point of comparison.

"So what are we looking at?" Brooke asked, her eyes on my wall of photos.

"Crime scene photos. I've got a client sitting in jail and a trial in three weeks. Take a look at this print of his neighborhood off Google Earth. See, here's the murder victim's house, and here, just around the corner, is my client's."

"Old Pit Bull Shorter."

"You're doing an injustice to pit bulls. Here's a close-up of the victim's house."

"Bill Hill. I like that name."

"It is short and pithy."

"I guess when he had a headache, his wife would say, 'Do you fill ill, Bill Hill?'"

"Chill, Bill Hill, and take this pill," I said. "But I don't think he was ever married. This is a picture of the murder scene. It looks like he was sitting in that upholstered chair when he was stabbed and fell forward onto the floor. Here's the dried pool of blood after they moved the body, soaking into the edge of the area rug and running out onto the wood floor."

"Shorter," she said. The word scrawled in blood stood in stark relief against a wood floor that had been worn almost white. She moved back to the photograph of the body lying facedown on the floor with one arm extended. "He was wearing a coat?"

"It was during the cold snap a couple of weeks ago. He didn't have his heat on."

"Gloves, too."

"Yeah, maybe he couldn't afford heat," I said.

"Have you been in the house?"

"Not yet. I thought I'd try to arrange it for this afternoon. Want to go?"

She did, and for once she had a break in her schedule that allowed her to do it.

Neither Hernandez nor his partner Jordan were available that afternoon.

"I can have a uniform meet you there at four o'clock," Hernandez offered. "Would that work?"

"Perfect."

"Maybe two uniforms. Their job will be to watch your hands at all times."

"Meaning that if I'm going to plant evidence, I need to be subtle?"

"Don't even joke about it, Starling. Any new evidence that's uncovered after you walk in that house, Biggs is going to claim you put there." Aubrey Biggs, Richmond's commonwealth attorney, was not my biggest fan.

"Then I hope you did an adequate job of searching when you had the chance," I said.

I was parked on the curb in front of Bill Hill's house when Jordan and Hernandez pulled up behind me in their SUV. Brooke and I got out.

"I thought you couldn't be here," I said.

"You didn't mention you were bringing company," Hernandez said.

Jordan added, "We got to talking it over and decided if you were going in that house, we needed to be here, too. You showing up with reinforcements just confirms our suspicions."

"Suspicions of what?"

"Of nefarious motives," Hernandez said.

"You know Brooke Marshall. She's my assistant," I said.

"She's your suite mate in the Ironfronts," Jordan said.

"Your best friend and your former roommate," Hernandez said.

"Well, today I've hired her as a consultant."

"You've hired her," Jordan said. "What are you paying her? I thought she did computer stuff."

"She does, but for her work today I'm planning to buy her dinner."

"Hey, that's good news," Brooke said.

Jordan shook his head. "Let's get this over with."

Bill Hill had been stabbed in his living room. We saw the chair he had fallen from, saw the stained carpet and the discolored wood flooring. Even the name of my client was still faintly visible on the old wood.

I had a printout of the house's layout I'd gotten off the city assessor's website and magnified with the executive suites' copier. Brooke, whose artistic talents exceeded my own, sketched in the major pieces of furniture as we walked through the house. Actually, all she was doing was putting labeled squares and rectangles on the page, which doesn't take a lot of artistic talent, but I was sticking with my strengths.

"I can't see what you're hoping to get out of this," Jordan said. "What are you looking for?"

"Don't know."

"Will you let us know when you find it?"

"If I know myself."

In the bedroom there was a machine next to Bill's bed, a plastic hose snaking out of it. I lifted the hose. A clear plastic mask with two black straps was attached to the end of it. "Did Bill Hill have sleep apnea?" I asked.

"Could be," Hernandez said. "I've got a buddy that uses one of those things."

"What's it called?"

"A BiPAP machine?" he suggested. "B-PAP?"

"C-PAP," Jordan said.

"Do you know?" I asked Jordan. "Or are you just guessing?"

"I've heard the term somewhere."

"Oo-kay." We weren't getting anywhere in a hurry.

I got out my smartphone and took a couple of snapshots of the clothes hanging in Bill Hill's closet and another shot of the two pairs of shoes and the ratty-looking pair of slippers lined up on the closet floor. I opened each drawer in his dresser to take a picture of its contents. In the bathroom was a little mirrored medicine cabinet, the mirror spotted with what looked like toothpaste.

"I had a medicine cabinet like this in my apartment when I was in law school," I said, opening it. Bill Hill had a lot of pills. After taking a picture of the contents of the medicine cabinet, I turned the bottles so that the labels faced out and took a couple of close-ups so I'd be able to read the labels.

Off the kitchen, an open staircase led down to a quarter basement with an oil furnace and a washer and dryer.

"This is a big waste of time," Jordan told Hernandez as we trudged single file back up the steps.

"Who knows what she'd have tried to pull if we weren't here?" Hernandez said. "And I didn't expect it to take so much time. I thought she just wanted to do a walk-through. I didn't know she was going to go Sherlock Holmes on us."

"So Jordan was in favor of sending the uniforms?" I asked, turning when I got to the top of the steps. "But Ray thought it needed the personal touch?"

"Ray was the one sparring with you on the witness stand the other day," Ray Hernandez said.

"Like I did my client any good." The kitchen was really too small for the four of us.

"I felt like I was faced off against a cobra. The whole time I was expecting a lethal strike."

"Sorry to disappoint." I held out my hand. "Well, I'm done here. Have I told you how much I appreciate this?"

"Not enough," Jordan said, taking my hand and giving it a squeeze that might have been a touch harder than necessary.

"Maybe you could buy us dinner, too," Hernandez suggested.

"Just you two, or do you think Mrs. Jordan and Mrs. Hernandez would like to come along?"

Neither one of them said anything to that. When we were out on the front walk again, I said, "I don't suppose we could walk over to Bob Shorter's house and do the same thing."

"You've got access to Shorter's house. You don't need us," Jordan said.

"I might need a witness if I find something."

"A couple of stooges is what you mean," Hernandez said.

Three kids were watching us from across the street about half a block down. They looked like high school students.

"What's your theory?" Jordan asked me. "You thinking Shorter killed Hill over there and then moved him?"

"My theory doesn't involve him killing Hill at all, but that's where the bloody clothing was found."

"And?"

"Maybe whoever planted it left traces."

Hernandez jerked his head in the direction of the teenagers down the block. "Who are they, do you know?" The tallest was a skinny kid with red hair, then there was a light-skinned black guy and a short white kid with dark hair and a round blob of a face.

I shook my head. "Never seen them."

"There weren't any traces," Jordan said, "because nobody planted the bloody clothes. We went over the place."

"Did you make an inventory of the contents of the house? Do you have pictures?"

"We have a few pictures of the closet where the bloody clothing was found."

"Yeah, I've seen those."

Hernandez said, "None of the house locks were broken. None had the telltale scratches on them that might suggest they'd been jimmied."

"Don't try to tell us you haven't already been in Shorter's house," Jordan said.

"Well," I admitted.

"So you know there are no indications that anyone other than Robert Shorter was ever in that house. None at all."

"Unless you found something we missed," Hernandez said, "and you're just not sharing it."

"Would it do me any good? If I came forward with a bit of exculpatory evidence, is there anyone in the police department or the DA's office who would believe I didn't plant it?"

"No," Hernandez said.

"Face it," Jordan said. "However good a job we did or didn't do of checking out Shorter's house, you're stuck with it."

Hernandez said, "And you don't really believe this theory of Shorter being framed by a person or persons unknown."

"He told me he didn't do it."

"It hasn't occurred to you that a person who would commit a murder would also lie about it?" Jordan asked.

"Sure, but he's my client. I have to explore the possibility that he's telling me the truth. I owe him that."

Jordan shook his head. "We did an inventory of the closet, if that helps."

They'd been more thorough than I had. "I don't think I've seen that. If you could send me a copy, I'd be grateful."

"How grateful?" Hernandez said.

Brooke said, "I thought you two were married."

"We are, but Jordan's not too happily."

Jordan held up a hand. "I'm very happily married," he said. "I'm ecstatic. Just ask my wife."

"Then let me ask you this," I said.

His head rolled toward me, and he looked at me from under his salt-and-pepper eyebrows.

"Shorter told me he kept a spare key in his toolshed. Do you know anything about it?"

"No, we don't. Given what the neighbors say about him, though, if someone was going to use his spare key, it would have been to go in and kill him."

"Or frame him. Can we check to see if it's there?"

If the key had ever been there, we couldn't find it. Hernandez, who had brought a flashlight from the SUV, shone it on the inside casing and all along the floor inside the shed. We saw a few empty nails, a few other nails with tools hanging from them, but no key. "Satisfied?" Hernandez said.

"Not really."

Jordan said, "I would say you'd removed the key last time you were here, but I can't see where it gets you."

I gave him a humorless smile. "If you figure it out, let me know."

Hernandez said, "I don't get it. I was expecting a key. I thought the whole reason you dragged us over here was because A, you'd planted it, or B, you'd already seen it, but you wanted us to be the ones to find it."

"I don't sense of lot of trust here."

"No, really? You gotta know we believe everything defense lawyers tell us."

Chapter 8

Hernandez and Jordan left. Brooke and I walked across the yard to Shorter's house. I wanted her to see the tombstones in the basement.

"Too bad it's not Halloween," I said, holding up the one about Jenn who died in her sin. "I'd put them out."

"You wouldn't."

"You saw what they did to my car."

She moved her head. "You aren't one to let a challenge go."

I worked the tombstone back into the crawl space. "That's hardly fair. I'm gentle Robin, meek and mild."

Her eyebrows drew together. "I've heard of gentle *Jesus*, meek and mild."

"I thought it sounded familiar. On the other hand, on one occasion this gentle Jesus drove a bunch of money changers out of the temple with a whip."

She laughed.

"I think of myself as gentle that way."

"Okay, you are gentle that way. But meek and mild?"

I shrugged, following her up the wooden steps from the basement. Brooke pushed open the door at the top of the steps, then fell back against me with a sharp yelp. I wasn't expecting it, and, but for a lucky grab at the rail, we might both have tumbled to the bottom of the steps.

"Good grief," I said, steadying her. "What's got . . ." The door at the top of the steps was standing open; the back door of the house was just beyond it. A distorted mask of a face was pressed against one of the door's glass panes, the mouth gaping. There were other faces beyond it, two of the teenagers we'd seen on the street, the redhead and the black guy, both of them grinning. The mask resolved into the face of the short, fat kid as he stepped back, his shoulders hitching up and down with laughter.

"Very funny," I called through the glass.

Pushing past Brooke, I stepped into the kitchen, and the fat kid lunged at the door. I don't think I flinched, but Brooke gave another squeal. "Let's get away from this door." I put a protective hand on her arm to guide her through the kitchen to the living room. I glanced back just before losing sight of the back door, but the boys were gone.

"Our car's parked in front of Bill Hill's house," Brooke said.

"Let's go back to Shorter's bedroom a minute. Maybe they'll wander off."

I planted myself squarely in front of the closet, trying to be open to anything that seemed out of place. I wished I'd made my own inventory when I was there before. What if I'd missed something?

"Robin?"

I held up a hand as I squatted in front of the closet to see under the hanging clothes. When I straightened, Brooke said, "Well?"

"Well what?"

"Did it work, going all mystical like that detective we used to binge-watch on TV?"

"Monk?"

"Monk."

"No. I guess I'm not obsessive-compulsive enough."

"Should we call your police friends?" Brooke asked. "Maybe they'd come back to give us an escort to your car."

"We can't do that." It was hard enough being a woman in a man's world, which criminal defense work still largely was.

"Why not?"

"Call out the Y-chromosome cavalry every time we get a little spooked?" I led her to the front door and picked up Shorter's ax handle from the corner. Resting it on my shoulder, I said, "Who needs 'em. Right?"

She looked at the ax handle.

"There's a gun back in the spare bedroom if you don't think this is enough."

She rolled her eyes. "Let's go."

There was no sign of the teenagers in the front of Shorter's house. I paused long enough to lock the dead bolt, then led the way down the erratically placed flagstones to the street. Shorter's lawn needed mowing. Though the weeds just grew in patches, some of them came up to midcalf on me—one more thing to irritate the neighbors, no doubt.

We saw the boys when we turned the corner. They were at my car, waiting for us, two of them sitting on the hood, the tall redhead leaning against it. His hoodie was up over his head now, and his bangs hung down over his eyes. Brooke and I stopped walking. Nobody said anything.

I brought Shorter's ax handle, which I'd been carrying discreetly against my right leg, back up to rest on my shoulder. The eyes of the pudgy kid on the hood of my car widened, and his gaze cut to the redhead.

"I see you've got Mr. Shorter's equalizer," the redhead said in a nasal voice. His hoodie was unzipped far enough to show the skull on his black T-shirt. "That's what he called it."

"What do they call you?" I asked him.

His lip curled. "Larkin."

"Hi, Larkin. I'm Robin Starling. This is my friend Brooke. She's a computer expert who has nothing to do with Bob Shorter and his troubles. Who are your friends?"

The pudgy kid was named Nate. The black guy was Warren. I didn't get any last names.

"You must be pretty desperate to meet girls," I said. "I have to tell you, though, this isn't the best way to go about it."

"I know something you don't," Larkin said. He pushed back his hoodie and shook his head, tilting it back to peer at me under his bangs.

"About meeting girls?"

"About Bill Hill and how Mr. Shorter killed him."

"Ah. What's that?"

"Wouldn't you like to know?"

I did want to know, so I waited.

"He did it, you know," Larkin said. "That man is as guilty as sin."

"Shorter? That's what the police say—the police, the neighbors, now you."

He leered at me from under his bangs, bobbing his chin.

"That's all you got?" I said. "Guilty as sin?"

His head stopped moving. "No, it's not all I've got. I got proof."

"Not just evidence but proof," I said. "That's good."

From the hood of my car, Warren said, "You think you're smart."

"Well," I told him modestly. My gaze went back to Larkin. "So what do you know that I don't?"

"Why should I tell you?"

"You want to, evidently. Why else are you here?"

"I'm gonna tell it to the police."

"Very good. You tell the police; they'll pass it along to me before the trial starts. That's the way it works. It's too bad you missed them, actually. They were just here."

"The police?" Nate said. "Those guys were police?" He looked at Warren.

"Told you," Warren said.

Larkin said, "They looked to me like they was working for you."

I shook my head, smiling at the thought of how very irritated Jordan and Hernandez would be to know that people had seen us together and formed the impression that they worked for me. "I wanted a look at the inside of Hill's house," I said. "They were here to make sure I didn't walk off with the silverware."

That got me a short bray of laughter from Nate, and a little tension went out of my shoulders. This was going to turn out okay.

Warren said to Brooke, "You're about the best-looking redhead I ever seen, and I like redheads. Brooke, is it?"

Okay, the tension was back. "Probably why you like to hang out with Larkin," I said.

Larkin's face flushed, and Warren scowled. *Way to de-escalate the situation, Robin.*

"It's time to tell me what you know or get off my car," I said, reaching into my purse with my left hand for the keys.

They stared sullenly and didn't move.

"Tell you what," I said and started toward my car, still talking. "I'll give your names to the police, let them know you've got important information. They'll find you, and you can tell them what you know." I beeped the car unlocked, my hand still in the purse that hung from my left shoulder. Larkin had stepped back a pace, apparently unhindered by his unlaced high-top sneakers. I hesitated before stepping to my car door and putting myself between Larkin and his friends. As I reached for the door handle, Warren slipped off the car to put his arms around Brooke, and Larkin stepped toward me, his arm reaching.

I reacted without thinking, bringing the ax handle down on Larkin's reaching forearm. The swing was too short to have a lot of force in it, but the ax handle caught his wrist, and he jerked his hand back. Nate had slid off the car next to me, and I brought the ax handle up to hit the inseam of his jeans. It wasn't a clean blow, hitting his thigh on the way in, but he did hunch over and put a hand to the hood of my car. I stepped around him, shifting my grip on the ax handle, but Warren and Brooke were already apart, Warren clutching his neck.

"She bit me," he said. "The crazy bitch bit me."

Behind me, Larkin said, "You're both crazy." I spun toward him, but he was holding his wrist and keeping his distance.

"You okay?" I said to Brooke.

She nodded. "Sure."

"Get in on this side. I think you need to drive." As she came around the car and got in, I stood protectively, the ax handle resting again on my shoulder. I handed her the keys, and she pulled the door shut. I walked around Nate, who was still hunched against my car.

"If you guys are going to mess with grown women, you're going to have to do something about your low pain thresholds," I said. Warren was standing in my way. Probably I should have gone around him, but I wasn't feeling accommodating. I lunged at him, causing him to step back into the shallow ditch that ran along the road in front of Bill Hill's yard and sprawl on the weedy clay that had been the lawn. I stepped over the ditch, looming over him, and he scrabbled crablike away from me on his hands and feet.

I stepped back across the ditch. Brooke already had the car going. I got in, and she pulled away while I was still shutting the door. She drove two blocks, turned the corner, stopped the car on the side of the road, and looked at me, her mouth twitching.

"What?" I said.

She started laughing, and I felt my own mouth twitching. "What?" I said again.

"You," she said. She wiped at the tears that were beginning to leak from the corners of her eyes. "You." But she was laughing too hard to go on.

Somehow the laughter was contagious. A burst of it escaped me with a sound midway between a snort and a honk.

"You've got to be the scariest female they ever hope to meet," Brooke said.

I stopped laughing. "What about you? How did you manage to bite Warren's neck when he'd grabbed you from behind?"

That set her off into a fresh storm of laughter. She pounded the steering wheel with the heel of her hand. "I'm a scary female, too," she squeaked.

That set me off again. The eyes of both of us were streaming before we got ourselves under control.

"Do I need to drive?" I said, wiping my cheeks with the heels of my hands.

She shook her head.

"What did happen with Warren?"

"You saw him grab me."

"Sure. That's what started everything."

"It wasn't anything dramatic. I turned against him, trying to get where I could push at him or knee him in the groin or something, but he was too strong and our feet weren't right. I lost my balance, and my face came down on the top of his shoulder. I was still trying to push away from him, but his neck was right there, so I bit it. That's when he let go."

I shook my head. "We are a crazy pair of females."

"Watch out, world," she said. She put the car in gear again, and we started off.

That was Monday. On Thursday, I received a letter from someone named John Hill, bar counsel for the Virginia State Bar, giving me thirty days to respond to the enclosed ethical complaint. There were two enclosures, actually. One was headed "Ethical Conduct Complaint" and began with Larkin Entwistle's full name and contact information. His occupation was student; he was still at Armstrong High School.

The next section, "Information about Attorney," had my name, office address, and phone number, but little else. When had he hired me? N/A. What had he hired me to do for him? N/A. What was his fee arrangement with me? N/A. I turned over the page to see the section titled "Explanation of Your Complaint":

> Ms. Robin Starling is representing the man accused of murdering Bill Hill, a disabled man in my neighborhood. She was in the neighborhood on March 26 of this year. I told her I had information about the case, that I had seen her client coming out of the murdered man's house on the day he was supposed to have been killed. She told me not to tell anyone, and she

threatened my friends and me with an ax handle. She said my whole family would be sorry if I went to the police, and that she personally would beat my brains out.

The complaint ended with a "List of Documents Attached: Cell Phone Photograph." It was a black-and-white print of a photograph that showed me standing with an ax handle raised over Warren, who was on the ground. The photograph was grainy and printed on copy paper like the rest of the complaint, but I was easily recognizable. I looked like a crazy woman.

Mike McMillan wiggled his fingers at me as he passed by my office door on the way into Brooke's office. A few minutes later, the two of them appeared in my doorway.

"Paul's going to meet us at the Marketplace," Mike said. "You ready to go?"

I was still holding the complaint, still thinking through its implications.

"Something wrong?"

I shrugged, tossed the papers onto my desk. Mike hesitated, but Brooke entered the office and picked them up. "It's an ethical conduct complaint," she told Mike. "A Larkin Entwistle filed it with the state bar." To me she said, "Is this the same Larkin who . . ."

I nodded. "Look at the picture."

She shuffled the pages. Mike stepped in to look at the document over her shoulder.

"Why were you beating a small black boy with a stick?" he asked.

"He wasn't as small as he looks."

Brooke said, "Ironically, he's the only one of the three she didn't hit with the stick. He's the one I bit in the neck."

"He's probably five nine or ten," I said. "About my weight."

"What do you mean, you bit him in the neck? What are you talking about? When did this happen?"

"Monday afternoon," Brooke said. "When I went with Robin to scope out the house of her latest murder victim. I told you about it."

"No, you didn't. You didn't say anything about biting someone in the neck."

"He's not *my* murder victim," I said. "I didn't kill anyone."

"It's kind of embarrassing," Brooke said. "I mean, biting someone in the neck. Besides you, I mean."

"Whoa," I said.

Mike shook his head as if to rearrange his mental furniture. "Let me see the complaint." He took the pages from Brooke and read the explanation, this time with Brooke looking over his shoulder. "How much of this is true?" he asked.

"None of it," I said, standing. "Well. I do represent the man accused of murdering Bill Hill. I was out there on Monday, and Larkin did tell me he knew something I didn't know. He didn't tell me what it was, though."

"And what about this picture?"

"That's what bothers me." I got my purse. "I didn't see anybody with a phone. Besides, when I was standing over Warren, the other two were behind me.

The angle's wrong." I looked over Mike's shoulder at the photograph, this time trying to picture the scene in three dimensions. "Melissa Stimmler," I said. "The woman who lives next door to Bill Hill's house. I bet this was taken through her picture window."

"Let's go to lunch," Brooke said. "All I had for breakfast was a cup of Greek yogurt."

We went to lunch, and we took the complaint with us. Paul read it as he slurped his smoothie. Theoretically, he was still trying to lose some weight, and every now and then he ate an inadequate lunch in service of the cause. I myself had a turkey and Swiss on whole wheat. It was a big sandwich, but I did forgo the chips.

"So how much trouble is this?" Paul asked, looking concerned.

"It's trouble," I conceded.

"What are you going to do?"

"I don't know. Respond to the complaint as requested. Something about it bothers me, though. Larkin's a seventeen-year-old kid. The average educational level of the adults in that neighborhood is maybe a year of community college and probably not even that. Read the first sentence: 'Ms. Robin Starling is representing the man accused of murdering Bill Hill, a disabled man in my neighborhood.' Larkin didn't write that. I've met his mother, Jenn, and I don't think she did, either. Nobody in that neighborhood is likely to think about going to the state bar with an ethics complaint anyway. Who are they going to call?"

"The police?" Brooke suggested.

I nodded. "And what are the police going to do?"

Mike said, "Well, since Larkin had evidence in a murder case . . ."

"Exactly. The police are going to take him to the office of the commonwealth's attorney."

"You think Aubrey Biggs wrote this complaint?"

"I do. His fingerprints are all over it."

"So he's finally got you," Paul said.

"No," I said. "He's finally gotten as far as filing a complaint."

"And you think you can beat it," Mike said.

"Well. I hope I can beat it."

"It's our word against theirs," Brooke said.

"Aubrey's got the picture," Paul said morosely. "That's what makes this so damaging."

Mike said, "Biggs may not stop with the complaint. Why would he? If you're threatening witnesses to keep Shorter from being convicted, you're an accessory after the fact. Ten to one he's going to charge you with a felony."

"Something to look forward to," I said. I put the last bit of my turkey sandwich into my mouth.

"At least it hasn't affected your appetite," Paul said.

"Nothing affects her appetite," Brooke said.

I stopped chewing, feeling suddenly like a pig at the trough.

Paul said to Mike, "Would it hurt your feelings if I canceled out on our trip?"

I swallowed. "What trip?"

Paul rolled his eyes.

"Boston, remember?" Brooke prompted me.

"Oh, yes. Of course." Mike was attending a conference held by the National Organization of Social Security Claimants' Representatives—NOSSCR for short—and Paul was going with him.

"Brooke ought to be the one going with you," Paul said. "And I hate to leave Robin right now."

"Don't be ridiculous," I said.

Mike said, "Brooke's name isn't the one on the plane ticket. I think it's you or nobody."

"Wow," Paul said. "And I'm better than nobody."

"Marginally," Mike said. "I would rather have Brooke, but when we planned this thing, she was just that beauty with the flame-colored hair who hung out with Robin."

Brooke's face flushed, but she looked pleased, I thought. Ol' Mike had just done himself some good.

Chapter 9

My visits to Shorter's neighborhood seemed to do me more harm than good, but I didn't have a lot of choice but to keep making them. Two o'clock found me on Melissa Stimmler's front stoop with my finger on the doorbell. I rang, and I waited. I rang again and waited some more. I sighed.

"Hey, Melissa, it's me again. Robin Starling, the lawyer everyone loves to hate."

No response. I rested my forehead against the door, operating on some vague notion that sound travels better through a solid than through air. "I'm for justice, no matter who it's for or against. Remember?"

In my defense, it had worked before. I turned away and sat on the top of her three steps, my forearms on my knees, to survey the neighborhood. My VW Beetle was parked on the road in front of Bill Hill's house next door, but, if it had attracted attention, it had not yet drawn anyone out of doors. The last thing I wanted was to get Melissa in trouble with her neighbors by advertising my presence at her house, but she wouldn't open her door to me, so here I sat on her front step in front of God and everyone. Of course, God knew where I was anyway, presumably.

Maybe five minutes had passed before I heard a sound behind me. I looked over my shoulder. The door was open a crack, the pale oval of a face visible in the shadows beyond the glint of the chain. I didn't get up.

"Hi, Melissa."

"Go away."

"I'm not the scary person everyone seems to think I am," I said. "Why can't we talk?"

"I saw what you did to those boys."

"I know. I got the picture."

She didn't say anything to that, which I took as confirmation that she had been the one to take the photograph.

"Did you see the whole confrontation, or just the end of it?" I asked. "I didn't start it. They were sitting on my car waiting for us, three teenage boys against two women. One of them grabbed my friend from behind. Another was trying to grab me. Did you see all that?"

I thought she wasn't going to answer, and when she did, she spoke so softly that I almost couldn't make it out.

"I saw," she said.

I waited.

"You had his stick. Mr. Shorter's."

"Yes. The boys had been leering at us through the windows of his house. I was hoping the sight of the stick would get them to leave us alone."

"He called it his equalizer."

"So I've heard. I didn't know about it then, though. How could I know it had such a bad reputation?"

I was addressing my comments more to the street than to her, not wanting to spook her by making eye contact. When I heard the rattle of the door chain, I turned. The door was standing open about a foot, but I no longer saw her in the opening.

I stood slowly, approached slowly, not wanting to startle her into hiding. In the doorway, I paused. "May I come in?"

"Please."

I stepped inside, feeling like a bull entering a china shop, all too aware that any movement might send the crockery tumbling. Melissa was standing so that she was shielded by the door.

"You know why he calls it his equalizer?" she asked from behind it.

"Was he afraid of the teenage boys in the neighborhood?"

"No."

"Dogs? Are there pit bulls and Rottweilers roaming the streets?"

"People's dogs get out sometimes."

"And Shorter's afraid of dogs?"

I wasn't sure whether she shook her head or had a brief seizure. "He doesn't like them." In a voice so soft it bordered on inaudibility, she added, "If they get too close . . . he hits them."

"Have you seen him do it?"

Melissa's eyes widened, but she didn't answer.

"Well, I won't carry his ax handle again."

She nodded, birdlike.

"May I?" I gestured toward the picture window and, when she didn't object, moved to it. She shut the door finally with a soft click and stepped after me, staying just outside of arm's reach as if I myself were a Rottweiler of uncertain temperament.

Her lawn sloped toward the street a little, and she had a view up the street in both directions. "Do Mr. Shorter's daily walks take him past your house?" I glanced at her. "You have a great perspective on the world here."

That observation triggered a small head movement that might have been a nod.

"When is the last time you saw Bill Hill and Bob Shorter together?" I asked. "Ever?"

She shook her head. "It's been years."

"What about the day of the murder, Friday the ninth—did you see Shorter go into Bill's house?"

"No."

"See him in Bill's yard?"

"I saw him that evening, just after dusk, walking and swinging his stick like always, but he stayed on the street."

It was her longest statement yet. Encouraged, I said, "You watched him pass Bill's house?"

"I did."

"And come back?"

"He doesn't come back. He makes a circle."

"Would you have seen him if he approached Bill's house from the back, through the alley?"

Her thin shoulders twitched. "Maybe, if I was in the kitchen. I didn't, though."

I nodded, thinking.

"I did see Bill in his yard that evening," she said.

"The Friday he was killed?" From somewhere back in the house came a shrill, thin whistle. "Is that . . ."

"Would you like some tea? I put the kettle on when I decided to let you in."

"Sure."

I followed her back to the kitchen. She took a battered-looking chrome kettle off the stove, and the whistle petered out. "I can offer you Earl Grey or Sleepytime," she said. "Sleepytime doesn't have caffeine. It's a mix of herbs—mostly chamomile but some spearmint, too, I think." She gestured with her head. "My window here looks out over Bill's backyard. I was washing some dishes when I saw him that night."

I looked over her head into Bill's small, square yard with its postage stamp of a patio and its single, sagging lawn chair. The pathology report had placed the time of death between noon and midnight. If Melissa had seen him alive in the middle of that twelve-hour window ... As she separated tea bags and dropped them into mismatched mugs, I asked, "What time was that exactly—do you remember?"

She poured on the water, and steam rose from the cups. She looked up at me, stricken. "I gave us both Sleepytime. I asked you what you wanted, but I didn't wait for your answer."

I smiled. "Sleepytime's fine. I'd like to try it."

She nodded, apparently relieved, and put a spoon into each. I started to ask her again about when she had seen Bill Hill, but she spoke first. "It was just starting to get dark. That would make it a little after seven, wouldn't it?" She squinted at me. "No, that was before the time change. It would have been a little after six."

"When was this in relation to when you saw Bob Shorter on his walk? Before or after?"

"Just before. It was darker when I saw Mr. Shorter but not completely dark."

"Did you see Bill Hill after that?"

She carried the cups to the small, Formica-topped table, and we both sat. "No. That glimpse I had of him through the kitchen window, it was the last time I saw poor Bill alive." She moved her tea bag around with her spoon, and I did the same. After a few minutes of mutual silence, she lifted spoon and tea bag onto a saucer she'd placed on the table between us. I lifted out my own and set my spoon next to hers.

"You seem to have run out of questions," she said. The wisp of a smile touched her mouth and then was gone.

That sounded like an invitation, but I refrained from pouncing. "I thought you might like to enjoy your tea in peace." I sipped from my mug.

"That's very considerate of you."

"Thank you. I'm afraid consideration isn't something I often get accused of."

"It's all right, though, if there's anything else you need to ask."

"Are you close to your neighbors? Jenn and Valerie and all the rest of them?"

"Not really." She looked sad to me. "I used to talk to Bill. I see Valerie Shaw sometimes, every couple of months or so. Have you met her?"

"Yes."

"She usually shouts whatever she has to tell me through the door. By the time I get it open, all that's left is for her to repeat herself."

"When the door's open and she's repeating herself, does she lower her voice?"

"Not much." That ghost of a smile touched her mouth again.

I nodded. "Valerie Shaw does have a voice on her." We sipped tea companionably a little longer. As I neared the bottom of the mug, mine was getting cold.

I said, "The reason I ask about your neighbors, I wondered how Larkin and his friends got that photograph of me with the stick. Did you call one of them, let them know you had it?"

She shook her head.

"Did they see you in the window?"

She looked as if she felt sick to her stomach. "Windows work both ways, I guess. That's always been the problem."

It sounded like a commentary on her life, but she didn't expand on it. "What happened?" I asked. "Did the boys come pound on the door until you opened it?"

She didn't answer, just looked at the table.

"And one of them snatched the camera out of your hands to see what you had?"

"My cell phone. Larkin Entwistle grabbed it and started scrolling through my photographs."

"Did he say anything?"

"He said, 'This is great, this is going to fix her,' or something like that. He texted the photo to himself before he would let me have my phone back."

I nodded. "The son of a gun."

"Yes. Son of a gun." Her tone carried a sudden tinge of viciousness, and I smiled at her. Tentatively, she returned the smile.

"It wasn't the only picture I took," she said. She took the phone out of the pocket of her housecoat and tapped the screen. She handed it to me.

I was looking at a picture of Warren with his arms around Brooke, clutching her from behind. The angle wasn't the best—I was looking at the two of them from the back—but it was clear he had her arms pinned. Just beyond them, Larkin was reaching for me.

"I don't want to do a Larkin on you. May I text this to myself?"

"Scroll back a picture. There's another one."

I slid my thumb across the screen. This photograph showed two boys sitting on my car, Larkin leaning against it, and Brooke and me stopped in front of them.

"You can have them both, if it will help."

I took a moment to send them to myself, feeling lighter of heart than I had since getting the notice from the Virginia State Bar. "I thank you for this," I said. "You can't know what it means to me."

When I stood to go, I noticed two bowls sitting on the floor at the end of the counter. They looked like dog dishes, but both were empty. "Do you have a dog?" I hadn't seen any other evidence of one . . . yes, I had. There had been a small cushion on the floor in the living room next to the recliner.

Melissa didn't respond immediately. I glanced at her.

"I used to," she said, still sitting at the table.

"I'm sorry."

"Her name was Nellie. Lymphoma took her. She was a little wire-haired dachshund."

"Those don't usually get cancer, I don't think."

"You know dachshunds?"

"My father was a veterinarian, and I helped him some. From a dachshund I would have expected back problems, maybe epilepsy or diabetes, but not lymphoma. I bet she barked a lot."

"She was a barker, but Bill Hill didn't mind, fortunately, and he's the only one who lived close enough to hear her." Melissa looked sad. "Dachshunds don't usually get along well with other dogs, you know, but she liked Buster. Buster was Bill's dog."

I sat back down across from her. "Bill Hill? I didn't know Bill had a dog."

"He used to. He died, too." It seemed that she was going to tell me something else, but if so, the impulse died without her adding anything.

I said, "Did the police ever question you about what you saw or didn't see on the day of the murder?"

"They came by, two men. One of them had on a tie."

"Did the one with the tie have a handlebar mustache?" I drew one on my face with an index finger. "And the other one a broad face, dusky skin, black hair?"

She gave one of her quick nods. "Hispanic, I think."

Jordan and Hernandez. "And you told them about seeing Bill Hill in his backyard that evening?" I asked.

"I didn't tell them anything."

"Why not?"

"I thought they might want me to testify. And I didn't see anything, not really, just a man sitting in his own backyard."

"It means Bill was alive at six o'clock. That's something we may not be able to establish apart from your testimony."

"They didn't say that. Does it matter? If he was killed before six o'clock or after?"

I didn't know. "Bob Shorter doesn't have an alibi for Friday evening, so maybe not."

She exhaled some of her tension and sipped her cooling tea.

"*Could* you testify, if I needed you?" I sipped my cold tea to give her time to think about it. Some of the tension had returned to her thin shoulders.

"I don't know," she said in a voice so soft I had to lean forward to hear it.

I studied her, a small, frail woman who might not top five feet in height. I didn't know if she could, either. She seemed broken in some way, and I wondered what events in her life accounted for it.

"I understand," I said.

I was in my car when I saw a yellow school bus letting off kids about a block and a half away: Four kids: Larkin, his two friends, and a girl with a chalk-white face and spiky, turquoise-colored hair. Warren and the girl turned away from me, her trailing him by half a dozen paces, both of their heads down and their eyes on the ground as they trudged along. Larkin and Nate came toward me, walking together, not talking. I put my car in gear and rolled forward, pressing the button that lowered the window.

Nate spotted me first and bumped Larkin's arm with the back of his hand. Both of them stopped. I brought the Beetle to a stop beside them.

"Hey, guys," I said.

Larkin said, "This is harassment. I'm going to report it."

"Who's your contact?" I asked. "Aubrey Biggs, the commonwealth's attorney, or somebody else?"

"I don't have to talk to you."

To Nate I said, "Did you and Warren see the same thing Larkin did, Bob Shorter coming out of Bill Hill's house on the day of the murder?"

Nate shot Larkin a glance. "I don't have nothing to do with that, man. I'm not involved."

"So you weren't all together that day, you and Warren and Larkin?"

"I don't have to talk to you."

"True enough." I shifted my attention to Larkin. "Must have scared the piss out of you, seeing Shorter coming toward you out of Bill Hill's house swinging that equalizer of his."

"Not just that. He had blood on him, too, all over his clothes."

"Did he? Splotches of blood, or were his clothes soaked with it?"

He just curled his lip at me. I heard a door slam, and a woman's voice loud enough to make me cringe, even at that distance. "Hey! What are you doing back here? You leave them boys alone."

I located Valerie Shaw in my side mirror, barreling down her sidewalk, her meaty arms pumping. I waved my hand out the window. "Just a friendly hello," I called. To Larkin and Nate: "You boys play nice."

I took my foot off the brake and rolled forward.

That evening, sometime after Deeks and I had finished our run, the music of Mozart was streaming through my TV's sound system. It was one of his operas, which I'm sure I would have enjoyed more if I understood German. I was dressed for bed in an oversize T-shirt and sipping my second glass of chardonnay—my second half glass, to be strictly accurate. Deeks was flaked out was on the cool tile in the foyer.

My mood was subdued. I would have appreciated company, but Paul had gone to Boston with Mike, despite his reservations. The next time Paul wanted to stay the night with me, I might just let him, I thought.

My phone began playing ABBA's "I Have a Dream," and I reached for it. "Hey, Brooke."

"Hey, Robin. How's it going?"

"All right. I was just wondering about the point of having a cuddly boyfriend if he's not going to be around to cuddle."

"I know what you mean. Have you ever been in Mike's house? You know where it is, don't you? In the Fan."

"I've driven by it. Paul's pointed it out."

"You wanna come over?"

"Are you there now? How come?" Brooke had her own apartment, and if she'd given it up and moved in with Mike, I hadn't heard about it.

"There's something I'd like you to see."

"What's wrong? You're not doing something weird, are you, going through his stuff?"

"Will you come?"

"Sure. Is Deeks invited?" I glanced in his direction, and he raised his head at the sound of his name.

"Of course. What's Mike gonna care about a little dog hair?"

"We'll be right there—well, there in twenty minutes or so."

She exhaled. "Thank you."

I punched off just as Deeks's cold nose touched my bare leg. He looked at me questioningly, which is to say his forehead wrinkled, and he had that worried look dogs get.

"Go for a ride?" I asked him. His forehead relaxed, and his tail began to wag.

I was quick. I pulled on some jeans under the oversize T-shirt, stepped into a pair of Top-Siders, and grabbed my purse. In less than five minutes we were backing out of the garage, Deeks turning around and around in the shotgun seat as he considered the most comfortable position in which to ride. He gave up about the time I got to the end of the alley and hopped between the seats to the back.

I adjusted my mirror to look at him. "Getting a little big for the front seat?" I asked him.

He lay down on the backseat with his front feet on the floor and his chin on the console between the front seats.

"I may have to get a bigger car," I said.

His tail thumped the side of the car.

"Materialist."

His tail thumped harder, but I think he just liked the sound of my voice.

Mike lived in a row house in the Fan, a district anchored on its narrower east end by Virginia Commonwealth University. Every morning, a city bus did a straight run down Grove Street, one block over from Mike's house, to Capitol Square, about a block away from my office and two blocks from his, convenient enough that he usually took the bus to work. In the evening it came back up his street and dropped him off about half a block from his house.

I found a parking spot against the curb across from the bus stop, and Deeks sprang between the seats into the shotgun seat. I looked at him, realizing that once again I had neglected to bring a leash.

"Stay close," I told him.

He wagged his tail and looked agreeable.

It was dark out, and there was no traffic on Hanover Street, but I held up a palm and said, "Stay. Be right back."

His tail stopped wagging, but he held his position as I opened my car door and got out. His obedience might have been helped by my keeping my hand up and almost in his face, but I like to think he was just well trained. I withdrew my arm and closed the door.

He stepped onto my seat and looked out at me, twisting himself as I went around the car to his door, which opened onto the curb instead of the street. "Stay close," I said through the window. I opened the door, and he hopped out onto the sidewalk beside me.

"Good boy. Stay close."

He went to check out the knobby sugar maple in a nearby tree well and found it interesting enough to pee on.

Brooke met us at the door wearing a man's dress shirt, her usually full hair almost flat, as if it had been combed out wet and left to dry.

"Have you been trying out Mike's clothes?" I asked. "Am I here to play dress up?"

"I was in the hot tub earlier, and I didn't have a cover-up. Hey, Deacon. How are you doing, you big, beautiful fur ball?"

He leaned against her as she scratched his neck, his back leg twitching. It had been months since I would have called him a fur ball. To me, he was beginning to look like a big, rangy dog. "You didn't tell me to bring my swimsuit," I said. The hint of a two-piece swimsuit was visible through the fabric of the white shirt. "I didn't even know Mike had a hot tub."

"Sorry. The hot tub would be a good place to talk after I show you what I have to show you. You can just wear your bra and panties, if you want to."

"Unfortunately, I'm only wearing half of that ensemble. I rushed out the door when you called."

She glanced at my chest. "Sorry," she said again. "Come see."

The house was narrow, no more than twenty feet wide, with exposed brick and green-painted drywall on the left and a light-wood paneling on the right. The living area furniture was modular, and about halfway back a set of stairs with a metallic rail led up to the second floor. I needed to start practicing Social Security disability law, I thought. It was evidently profitable to receive checks issued by the US Treasury on a regular basis.

A pullout desk was built into the right wall just behind the staircase. "Here," Brooke said. "Look."

A fat, unabridged dictionary lay open on the desk. Deeks sniffed at the edge of the desk, but he lowered his nose when he didn't smell food and trotted back into the living room to check it out more thoroughly.

"Keep your leg down," I called after him. "What?" I said to Brooke.

"Isn't he house-trained?"

"Oh yeah. It's been weeks since he's gone in someone's house."

She rolled her eyes. "Here. Look at the slip of paper."

It looked like the corner of a sheet of copy paper tucked into the crease between the pages of the big dictionary. I picked it out. On it was written, in a looping script, "I love you."

She handed me two more scraps of paper. They said the same. "They were all in the dictionary, marking pages where the words *love*, *sex*, and *forever* were highlighted. Come on back."

I followed her into the galley-style kitchen at the back of the house. On the table were half a dozen books or so, all of them lying open, all with scraps of paper tucked between the pages. I picked out one of the scraps and turned it to read the writing: "I love you." It's what they all said.

"You didn't write these, I take it," I said.

"You know I didn't. Sarah did this, that Sarah Fleckman, and she left them scattered through Mike's books."

"All of them?"

"No, not all of them, but enough. He's going to be running across them for the rest of his life."

I picked up one of the books to look at the cover: *Harry Potter and the Half-Blood Prince*. Another book was *The Fellowship of the Ring*. Another was the Bible, which was open to the Song of Solomon.

She flipped a slimmer volume shut and held it up so I could see the spine. "He'll be reading *The Magician's Nephew* to our children one day, and right in the middle of chapter six he'll run across one of these little love notes from Sarah Fleckman."

"You've already talked about having children?"

She gave me a look.

"Maybe Mike wrote them," I suggested. "Maybe he left these notes for you."

She made a dismissive sound. "Why would I be reading Mike's books?"

"Why would you be wearing his shirt?"

"Besides, it's not his handwriting."

"But you don't know it's Sarah's. Maybe they're love notes from his mom."

"With *sex* highlighted? It's Sarah Fleckman—you know it is. Did you know she tricked him into meeting her for lunch last week? Wouldn't tell him what it was about, just that it was important. Then when he got there, she told him she was in a different place in her life, and now she was ready to get married."

"Mike told you about it?"

"Yes." After a moment, she shrugged. "And that was good. He's not keeping secrets from me."

"How did you happen to run across these love notes?"

"I was looking up *expatiate*."

"Expatiate? How come?"

"I was talking to Mike on the phone, and he said something about sitting through the opening session of his conference, listening to one person after another expatiate. I didn't want to ask him what it meant."

"You didn't Google it?"

"He's got this big, fat dictionary sitting right here on his shelf."

"How long ago do you think she wrote them? Probably it's been months. It could have been a year or more."

"You see what that means, don't you? When he runs across one, he tucks it right back into his book. He's keeping them for sentimental reasons."

"You don't know how many he's run across and thrown away. She might have written hundreds."

"Great. The house is infested with them."

"It is a great house, though," I said.

"I know. Isn't it?" She looked up at the twelve-foot ceiling, her expression wistful.

"It's not ruined for you, either, not the house and not Mike's library. It's just going to take you a while to make them your own."

She nodded, her lips compressed, her expression thoughtful.

"Come on," I said. "Let's do the hot tub."

"You're just going to . . ." She waved a hand.

"I'll keep my shirt on. I'm sure Mike has another one I can borrow."

Deeks did not like the hot tub with its noisy jets and the steam coming off the surface of the roiling water. He backed up growling when Brooke flipped the cover back, then began to whine anxiously as we climbed into it. I relaxed against the wall of the tub, resting my forearm on the side, and Deeks's mouth closed on my wrist.

"Hey," I said.

He tugged at my arm, but I disengaged myself and pushed at his head. "Go check out the yard," I said. "It's unexplored territory."

"Dig something up," Brooke suggested.

I looked at her. "You're not yet thinking of this place as your own."

"It isn't yet my own."

Deeks sat on the deck by the tub, watching us. He gave me a whine.

"You're such a mother hen," I told him. To Brooke I said, "Set a wedding date. The house'll be yours before you know it."

"Shouldn't I wait until this thing with Sarah Fleckman is resolved?"

I wished Deeks would stop whining. "It is resolved," I said. I pushed at my T-shirt, which kept floating to the surface of the water. "Look, there are two possibilities. One, Mike can't be trusted around other women. If that's true, the thing to do is break off the engagement and stay as far away from him as you possibly can."

"And the other possibility?"

"Is that he can be trusted. And if that's the case, you need to trust him."

She nodded, but she didn't look happy about it.

"Is there something in your past that makes trust difficult for you, something I don't know about?"

She didn't say anything.

"I mean, I know I have trust issues," I said, "but my father left my mother and ran off with his veterinary assistant."

"And you had a boyfriend who cheated on you. John Parker."

Nice of her to remind me. "So what's your excuse?"

She took a breath. "Just a character flaw, I guess."

Deeks's jaws close on my forearm again, and I turned my head to meet his wrinkled-forehead gaze. "You can't just relax, can you?" I said to him.

"I guess that's my problem, too," Brooke said.

"Yes, yes, it is. The two of you just need to relax. Take a chill pill, why don't you."

Chapter 10

By the time the trial date rolled around, I was ready for it—not in the sense of having developed any exculpatory evidence, but at least in the sense of not being able to think of anything else I could do that was likely to help. I still hadn't filed my answer to Larkin's ethical complaint. My deadline for that was five days away, which, according to Paul, meant I wouldn't be working on it for another four and a half days at least. "I'm not making a personal criticism," he said. "I'm just noting that you're an attorney. Attorneys never do anything until the last minute."

"There's a reason for that," I told him. "Cases settle all the time. They settle, and they get postponed. You do a lot of work ahead of time, too often it's wasted."

"Hard work may pay off some day—procrastination pays off now," he said.

"Exactly."

"So what happens today?" Shorter asked me as we waited for the trial to get started.

"Jury selection."

"That's it? Jury selection?"

"Maybe opening statements. If the prosecution gets to call a witness, though, I'll be dumbfounded."

"I can't say that's very comforting."

"That the wheels of justice take so long to get turning?"

"That my attorney's going to be dumbfounded."

I shrugged.

"So what have you come up with?" he asked.

I shook my head. "Nothing."

"What do you mean, nothing? What have you been doing with your time?"

"Spider solitaire."

His face darkened.

"Only kidding. I've made myself familiar with the facts associated with the case, and I've spent more time thinking about them than you can imagine."

"Oh, goody. You've been thinking."

"One of your neighbors saw you leaving Bill Hill's house on the day of the murder. Did you know that?"

"Who?"

"Does it matter?"

"It's a lie," he said.

"Sure. Why not?"

"What do you mean, why not?"

"You say you weren't in Hill's house, but you would say that, wouldn't you? You want to get acquitted. They say you were there, because they want to see you convicted."

His eyes narrowed.

"Maybe one of you is lying, but what difference does it make? Each of you is telling a story designed to lead to the desired result. That's the rational thing to do, isn't it?"

"You wouldn't know rational if it bit you on the butt. For one thing, one of us is obviously lying. I can't have been seen coming out of Bill's house if I was never in there, and I must have been in there if I was seen coming out. Don't they teach logic in law school?"

"Castles in the air," I said.

"What's that?"

"That's what they teach us. How to build castles in the air."

Jury selection took most of the first day. I didn't try to accomplish anything subtle. My goal pure and simple was to keep women off the jury. Although Shorter wouldn't be testifying—that would be catastrophic—several of his neighbors were on the witness list. I didn't think it would take much of their testimony to poison the women in the jury to the point that it would be difficult for them to evaluate the case objectively. Don't get me wrong: Bob Shorter was unpleasant, obnoxious, and quite possibly evil, and it wasn't going to be any easier to hide that from the men. My hope was that the men might take it a little less personally.

So. I didn't want any women, but I got three, which gave me a bad feeling about the outcome of the trial right from the beginning. When the jury had been impaneled, Ian Maxwell's opening statement was brief, suggesting the strength of his case: William Hill was found dead in his residence on March 11. He had been stabbed with a knife bearing the defendant's fingerprints. A search of Robert Shorter's house had uncovered clothes with blood on them: the clothes were in Shorter's closet, pushed back underneath his hanging clothes, where they were hidden from view. DNA tests had shown the blood to be not Bob Shorter's blood but Bill Hill's. "Most damning of all, the murder victim had, in the last moments of his life, used his finger to write a name on the floor in his own blood. The name he wrote was one word: Shorter." Even though nothing Maxwell said in his opening statement was evidence on which the jury could base its verdict, the case he outlined sounded pretty open-and-shut.

"What about motive?" Maxwell asked the jury. "Here we come to what is perhaps the strongest part of the commonwealth's case. Certainly, motive is a more prominent element of this case than of any case I have ever prosecuted."

Okay, that was too much. I stood. "I hate to interrupt the prosecutor's personal reminiscences," I said, even though of course that was exactly what I wanted to do. "But we've got a relevance problem here. What does Mr. Maxwell's lack of experience in prosecuting cases have to do with the guilt or innocence of this defendant?"

Circuit Judge Benjamin Cooley, an elderly old coot who'd been on the bench since the Carter administration, said in a voice that quavered only slightly, "*Is* your lack of experience relevant, Mr. Boxwell?"

Maxwell was probably younger than I was, maybe still in his twenties. He wore round-lensed glasses, and his scalp showed pink through his close-cropped blond hair. "Maxwell, Your Honor. No. I wasn't talking about my lack of experience, but about the strength of the evidence showing motive."

"I don't want to criticize the way you're beginning your case, but wouldn't it be better to actually talk about that evidence?"

Maxwell took a breath. "Yes, Your Honor."

"I'll sustain the objection, then. Proceed, Mr. Maxim."

Maxim wasn't his name, either, but he let it go. "Members of the jury. This killing was motivated by the animosity between this defendant and his victim. And it was not the first time that the defendant had harmed Bill Hill. He and Mr. Hill used to be friends, but some years ago they ceased to be friends. They became, in fact, enemies. Just how serious that hatred was and how it came about will become apparent as the trial proceeds. I know you will evaluate the evidence impartially and fairly. You will find not only that the defendant killed Mr. Hill, but that it was a deliberate, willful, and premeditated killing. In short, you will find beyond a reasonable doubt that the defendant Robert Shorter is guilty of murder in the first degree."

As Ian Maxwell took his seat, Judge Cooley looked at the clock. "I see that we've passed the hour for adjournment," he began, and I stood.

"Ms. Sterling?"

"It's Starling, Your Honor. The jury at this point has heard only one side of the story. It would be unfair to have them retire for the night without also hearing from the defense."

Judge Cooley's eyes drifted back to the clock on the wall, his expression wistful.

"I'll be brief, Your Honor," I promised.

"All right, Ms. Starling. Your opening statement."

I went to the lectern. I smiled, making eye contact with several members of the jury, with all of them who would look at me. "I'm standing between you and your dinner, and I'm sorry," I said. "As legal counsel for a man accused of the most serious of crimes, it puts me in an uncomfortable position. The judge will instruct you that you're not to talk about this case among yourselves or with anyone else, that you're not to form any conclusions as to the guilt or innocence of the defendant until you have heard all the evidence—but we're human. Our minds dwell on the questions that confront them, weighing the available evidence either consciously or unconsciously. Before you go to your dinners, I want you to know one thing. There are two sides to the case. Some of the evidence may be incontrovertible—DNA evidence linking the blood on the clothes found in the defendant's house to the blood of the victim, the fingerprints on the knife in the victim's house . . . but even there I urge you to evaluate the evidence critically. The law wraps Mr. Shorter in a cocoon of innocence, and before he can be convicted of a crime—any crime—the prosecution must peel away the presumption of innocence piece by piece and layer by layer until not a shred of it remains.

"Suppose the DNA evidence and fingerprint evidence do hold up. It's not the end of the story. We still need to consider how a knife from Mr. Shorter's kitchen, if it came from there, came to be in the victim's house. There might be innocent explanations—perhaps Mr. Shorter lent him the knife so that it was there in the house for the murderer to pick up—or there might be explanations that are a good deal more sinister. Many of us have left a key to our homes with a neighbor or even hidden somewhere on our property so that we don't have to break a window if we're ever locked out. Anyone who knew about such a key could walk into Mr. Shorter's house and walk out again with a knife and a few items of clothing. After the murder, the killer could write the name of everyone's least favorite neighbor in the dead man's blood. He could leave the knife and take the bloody clothing, enter one more time into Mr. Shorter's house, and there you have all the evidence of the prosecution's case."

There it was in a nutshell, the only viable theory of a case for acquittal, the theory that Bob Shorter had been framed. I had presented it as matter-of-factly and prosaically as possible. Now I paused to consider whether I should deal directly with the common tendency to dismiss allegations of manufactured evidence as the product of nut-job conspiracy theorists. I decided to let it go.

"You're going to hear evidence that Mr. Shorter is not a very nice person. I don't know what that has to do with the question of whether or not he committed the particular crime he is accused of, but you're likely to get the idea that Bob Shorter is one malicious SOB." I paused again to look at Bob Shorter. The jury looked at Bob Shorter. He bared his nicotine-stained teeth at them. He was wearing rumpled chinos and a light jacket over a polo shirt, which, combined with his yellow teeth, oily hair, and prominent hooked nose, made him look like Lucifer's indigent second cousin. I should have foreseen this moment and gotten him some nice clothes and some dental work done, but there was nothing I could do about it now.

I said, "Please keep in mind that even if we come to dislike Mr. Shorter, even if we come to despise him, there are a lot of malicious SOBs out there who have never killed anybody. Our job, your job, is to evaluate the evidence that ties this particular murder to this particular SOB. And the tie has to be a strong one. There can be no other reasonable explanation for the facts the prosecution is able to establish. If there is, it is your obligation to acquit."

It was probably not my strongest opening statement. I had dinner with Brooke and Mike and Paul that evening, and they confirmed my doubts. We were at Enrique's, a Mexican restaurant we like, eating chips and salsa. Brooke and I were sipping margaritas, and Paul was drinking a mug of a draft beer I had never heard of, when Brooke said, "Something seems different about this case. Are you sure you have your heart in it?"

She and Mike had gotten to court just as Maxwell started his opening argument, and Paul had gotten there just as I started mine. "He's an SOB," Paul said, lifting his mug, "but he may not be a murdering SOB."

"Damning him with faint praise," Brooke said.

"Having an unsympathetic client is the big weakness in my case," I said. "I'm afraid Shorter's going to look uglier and uglier as the trial progresses. I thought I'd better strengthen my credibility with the jury by acknowledging that up front."

Paul asked, "You think the unsympathetic client is a bigger liability than the bloodstained clothes and the fingerprints on the murder weapon?"

"Not to mention the defendant's name written in the victim's blood," Brooke said.

"Well, none of that helps," I acknowledged.

"What did Shorter think of your tactic?" Brooke asked.

"Not much."

"He didn't comment?" Mike said. "I saw you talking to him."

"It would be more accurate to say you saw him talking to me. Specifically, he said he should have known better than to put his life in the hands of a ditzy blonde female with poop for brains."

They looked at me.

"He said that?" Paul asked. "Poop for brains?"

"No, he was a bit earthier in his description, but I think we all get the point."

"I'm afraid you're going to lose this one," Paul said.

"Maybe," I said. "Nobody bats a thousand. I lost a few cases when I was on the civil side of the docket, too."

"Out of how many?" Mike asked. "How many jury trials did you have before you got into criminal defense work?"

I shrugged. "Here comes the food. Believe it or not, after a day in court I don't find my professional shortcomings a relaxing topic of conversation."

"Point taken," Paul said. When the waitress had distributed our food, Paul pointed to me. "This lady would like another margarita," he said.

"So would this one," Brooke chimed in.

For the rest of the evening we talked of other things, but I never felt completely in the moment. My mind kept drifting back to Bob Shorter, who I was pretty sure would have killed Bill Hill if he had felt like it. My doubts about him didn't provide much basis for a wholehearted defense.

I was in bed by ten, but my cell phone rang shortly before midnight, David Gates singing, "Baby, I'm-a Want You." I groped for the phone, tapped the glowing screen.

"Hey, Paul."

Beside me on the bed, Deeks came to his feet.

"Robin. Are you awake?"

"More or less. Someone just called me in the middle of the night and woke me up."

"Sorry. It couldn't be helped. Mike and I are on our way over."

"What?" I pushed up in bed. "Is everything all right? What happened?"

I heard Mike's voice next: "We'll tell you when we get there. See you soon."

The call ended, and I rested the phone against my chest. Deeks touched his cold nose to my cheek, and I worked a hand into his fur. "Hey, buddy. We got company coming." I pushed my legs out of the covers and sat for a moment on the side of the bed as Deeks leaped lightly to the floor.

"Show-off," I muttered, then sighed and got up. In the dark, I rummaged in a drawer for some gym shorts to pull on over my panties. I thought for a moment, then opened the top drawer to find a bra. If it was just Paul, I probably wouldn't have bothered— let him get hot and bothered if he wanted to—but I didn't want to spend an evening with two men glancing surreptitiously at my chest.

"I don't know what it is with men and mammaries," I told Deeks, shrugging into the bra beneath my oversize T-shirt.

His tail thumped against the side of the bureau, and I reached down to scratch his head. Then I got the water bottle off my nightstand and opened it on my way to the living room.

"You need to go potty?" I asked Deeks, standing in front of the picture window.

He barked and wagged his tail, so I opened the front door. Paul hadn't given me much warning. His car pulled up just as Deeks was finishing his business.

Mike got out, wearing rumpled jeans and an even more rumpled T-shirt. Paul was wearing sweats. Deeks greeted each in turn on their way to the door, a bounce in his step and his tail wagging, clearly more excited than I was about the nighttime visitors. I do have to admit to being intrigued, but I waited until they were standing awkwardly in my living room before I said anything.

"Can I offer either of you a hot beverage?"

It didn't even get a smile.

"Is it Brooke?" I asked Mike.

"No. She's fine."

Good news. I sat on the sofa, curling my legs under me, and Paul and Mike sat, too.

"It's Sarah," Mike said, his elbows on his knees and his fingers laced in front of him.

"Sarah Fleckman? Something's happened to Sarah Fleckman?" He was never going to disentangle himself from that woman, I thought.

"Not exactly. She . . . let herself into my house. She was there when I got home from Enrique's."

Mike's story was that he had parked on the street and let himself in through the front door, dropping his briefcase by the sofa on his way back to the kitchen to set up the coffeemaker so his morning coffee would be ready by the time he got downstairs. He'd gone to his bedroom, had hung his suit up in the closet, had tossed his shirt on the floor underneath his hanging clothes, which evidently was where he kept clothes that needed to go to the cleaners. Wearing boxer briefs and a T-shirt, he had gone into the bathroom to brush his teeth and wash his face. He hadn't known anything was amiss until he'd gotten into bed and a warm, naked female had pulled herself against him.

"Wait a minute," I said. I'd been to his house now and knew the layout. "You went in and out of your bedroom, into your closet, into your bathroom, and you never noticed there was someone in your bed?"

"All I noticed was a jumble of covers. I don't always make my bed."

I rolled my eyes. Brooke, I knew, couldn't stand an unmade bed, which told me who was going to be making theirs.

"Anyway, I broke free of her and got out of bed."

"Got out of bed!" Paul said. "He launched himself out of bed like his sheets were on fire." To Mike he said, "What? It's the way you told it to me."

"Let's just say I got out of there as fast as I could. I was halfway down the stairs before I realized I didn't have anything on but my underwear. I had to run back up and snatch some clothes off the floor."

His house had been so neat when Brooke showed me through it. I wondered if she'd picked up after him, or if he did better when he was going to be away.

"And Sarah was still there, I take it?"

"She was out of bed at that point. I had to move her to get to my clothes."

"And she was still . . ."

"Still wearing the clothes she was born in," Paul said. He seemed to be relishing the mental image of a naked Sarah a good deal more than was strictly proper for a boyfriend of mine.

"She still hasn't given you up," I told Mike.

"The weird thing is, she says she has," Mike said. "Evidently what she had in mind was something of a good-bye present."

"A thank-you for all the good times they had," Paul said.

"Must have been some good times," I said drily. "So how did you leave it?"

"I just left it, the house and everything."

"He can't even remember if he locked the front door," Paul said.

"Sarah will lock it when she leaves," Mike said.

"How come she still has a key?" I asked.

He shook his head. "She gave it back to me a long time ago. Evidently, she'd made a duplicate she never told me about."

"So what's your plan?"

"Sleep at Paul's tonight. She'll be gone in the morning."

"At some point she has to go to work," Paul said.

"No, I meant, what are you going to do about Sarah's unbreakable attachment to you?" I said.

"I thought maybe you could talk to her," Mike said.

And there it was. That was why they were here. "You have to change your locks."

"I know. Tomorrow morning."

"And this is another thing you have to tell Brooke about."

Mike glanced at Paul. "She'll freak out. You know she will. She'll be over at my house washing sheets and wiping down everything in sight."

"You don't plan to wash your sheets?"

"Well, sure. Eventually."

"Good grief."

"I know, I know. Brooke's got to know about it. For one thing, after I've changed my locks, she'll need a new key to the house. I did think I might leave out some of the details as to why."

"Details like Sarah being naked," Paul said. "And in his bed, waiting for him like a bare-breasted spider."

My lip curled as I turned my gaze toward him. "Is that a new species?"

"As of tonight," he said. "I took the privilege of naming it."

"Even though I'm the one who discovered it," Mike said.

"I thought you wanted to keep that part of things quiet," I said.

"Good point."

I shook my head. *Men and mammaries*, I thought. *Men and mammaries.*

Chapter 11

The next morning Mike had back-to-back hearings in the federal building across the street, and Paul had to go to Norfolk for some reason. Only Brooke was there when court reconvened and Ian Maxwell called Mark Rehrer, whom I had last seen in Shorter's kitchen, as his first witness.

"Old man Rehrer" turned out to be fifty-six, an age consistent with his white side walls and the coal-black strip of hair that ran back from his forehead. Though Shorter's tombstone had suggested he got the electric chair for cutting his wife from ear to ear, he currently lived with his unmurdered wife across the street from the house that had belonged to Bill Hill.

"Did you see Mr. Hill from time to time?" Maxwell asked him after going through the preliminaries.

"Yes, occasionally."

"You knew him fairly well?"

"I knew him to talk to. He had problems walking, though, and he rarely left his yard."

"What gave him walking problems?"

"The front half of one of his feet had been amputated six or seven years previously."

"Did you see him on the day of Friday, March 9?"

"No."

"Did you see him on Saturday, March 10?"

"No. Saturday night, though, the light in Bill's living room was on all night. At least, it was on when I went to bed Saturday night and still on when I went out to get the newspaper before daylight the next morning."

"This was unusual?"

"Yes. Bill was usually up pretty early, but he went to bed early, too. I hadn't seen him for a while, and later that day I got to thinking about it. I thought maybe his light had been on all Friday night, too."

"How often did you see him normally?"

"At least every day or two. Bill didn't get out much, but he did run to the grocery store every few days. And he'd shuffle out to his mailbox. Mostly, though, I'd see him in his backyard or at his front window, looking out at the neighborhood and brooding."

"What did Bill Hill have to brood about?"

I stood. "Objection. Relevance." Some of this could come in as part of the res gestae, the circumstances surrounding the case, but Maxwell looked to be heading into things I didn't want him heading into.

"Sustained," Judge Cooley said. To Maxwell he added, "I'm not sure where you're going with this, but you need to get to the point."

"Very well. Mr. Rehrer. Was the defendant Robert Shorter responsible for Mr. Hill losing part of his foot?"

"Objection," I said again.

Maxwell turned to me. "You can't argue the relevance of that one. If Bob Shorter—"

I interrupted him. "Whatever Bob Shorter may or may not have done might be relevant if you could prove it by competent evidence, but I'm betting that all Mr. Rehrer knows about the matter is what somebody told him."

Maxwell hesitated, which was fatal.

"Are you attempting to solicit hearsay evidence, Mr. Maximus?" the judge asked him in his quavery voice.

"Maxwell. I'll be calling the physician who treated Mr. Hill at a later time, Your Honor."

"Let's wait for that testimony then," the judge said. "I'll sustain the objection."

Maxwell adjusted his glasses. "Mr. Rehrer," he said, "what did you do on Sunday, March 11, in relation to Bill Hill?"

"Nothing until the afternoon, I'm afraid. A bit before two o'clock, I walked across to ring his doorbell. Bill didn't answer, so I got down off the stoop and looked in his picture window. When I stood on tiptoe, I could see his legs. He was on the floor. I knocked on the glass and shouted to him, but he didn't move, so I called nine-one-one."

"You didn't try the door?"

"No. I didn't."

"Thank you, Mr. Rehrer." To me: "Your witness."

The more time Mr. Shorter's neighbors spent on the stand, the worse it was going to be for Mr. Shorter, I thought. "No questions," I said.

"Call Officer Steven Warren," Maxwell said.

Officer Warren had been the first cop on the scene. He rang the doorbell and knocked and tried the door. "It wasn't locked," Warren said. "So I went in. A man was lying facedown on the floor in front of a recliner. It looked like maybe he'd been stabbed in the chair and fallen forward."

"It looked like he had been stabbed? Did you see a weapon?"

"I saw a small knife on the floor by the decedent's body."

"Did it have blood on it?"

"It was at the edge of a pool of blood that was only partly covered by the dead man's body. The blade was smeared with blood."

"Anything unusual about the crime scene that you noticed?"

"There was a pattern in the blood that looked like writing. It was a word, but not one I understood until later."

"What was the word?"

"Shorter."

Maxwell turned to look at the members of the jury, emphasizing the importance of that one word. "Shorter, as in Robert Shorter?" he asked the witness.

"Objection," I said. "Leading." Lawyers aren't allowed to ask their own witnesses questions in ways that suggest the answer. Of course, everyone knew that Shorter was the defendant's name, but I saw no reason to let Maxwell wallow in it.

"Sustained," the judge said.

Maxwell spent an inordinate amount of time turning pages on his yellow pad. Finally he looked up and asked, "Was the word Shorter written in all capitals?"

"The *S* was. Well, it was as tall as the vertical line of the *H* beside it. All the other letters were little letters."

"Lowercase letters?"

"Yes. Lowercase."

"What did you do next?"

"I didn't do anything," Warren said. "I called it in and waited for Homicide."

"Your witness," Maxwell told me.

I half stood. "No questions."

Shorter flapped his hand at me, his expression suggesting he'd been sucking on a lemon. I leaned toward him.

"When are you going to question one of these witnesses?"

"When I think it will do us some good," I said.

"Well, I didn't pay you thirty thousand dollars to sit there on that scrawny little butt of yours."

"I'm sorry," I said. "I must have misunderstood."

Maxwell was calling his next witness, a doctor named Rosen. Shorter's hand closed on my forearm, the strength of his grip suggesting he hadn't appreciated the levity of my response.

I tilted my head toward him, smiling as pleasantly as I could with warm breath that smelled overpoweringly of stale tobacco caressing my face. In a low voice I said, "Create a scene here in front of the jury, and you're going to spend the rest of your life in prison. There won't be a thing you or I or any other lawyer can do about it."

He let go of my arm, and the reek of his breath receded.

Dr. Rosen had come to the witness box wearing a sports jacket and tie that seemed a little dressy for his rumpled chinos and battered, brown athletic shoes. He had dark, curly hair that was just beginning to gray.

"Could you state your name for the record?" Maxwell asked him.

The doctor could. He was an ER doctor at Chippenham Hospital who had been on duty one night eight years ago when William Hill came in with frostbite in his hands and feet.

"How did you know it was frostbite?"

"Symptoms and patient history."

"What were the symptoms?"

"Fever, intense shivering, slurring of speech. Patches of his skin were hard and waxy in appearance and grayish yellow in color. I'm referring specifically to the skin on his chin and his nose and his fingers and toes, including most of his right foot."

"And the patient history?"

I stood up. "Your Honor? May counsel approach the bench?"

Judge Cooley's head bobbed on his thin, wattled neck. "You may approach."

As Maxwell and I went forward, the court reporter moved closer and pushed the button that turned on the white noise designed to keep the jury from hearing our bench conference. I had asked for one because I didn't want the jury to know I was trying to keep them from hearing relevant evidence. Juries don't like that.

"Your Honor," I said. "What the witness is about to give us is hearsay, something the decedent told him or told a hospital nurse many years before his death."

Maxwell said, "It was a statement made for medical diagnosis or treatment. That's a clear exception to the hearsay rule."

"What's the prosecution trying to prove by this testimony?" I asked the judge. "Not that Bill Hill had part of his foot amputated because of frostbite."

"What I'm trying to prove is that this isn't the first time the defendant tried to kill him."

"Exactly," I said. "The defendant's name is going to come out of this doctor's mouth, and that name had nothing to do with the patient's condition or his course of treatment."

"It falls within the exception to hearsay, Your Honor."

"It's highly prejudicial and not especially reliable. I can't cross-examine Mr. Hill about who he said was responsible for his condition. He could have had a grievance against Mr. Shorter or some other reason for not being truthful about the events that led to his frostbite. He came in with frostbite. That's all this witness can tell us of his own knowledge."

The judge turned his gaze to Maxwell, who shrugged. "It falls within the exception, Your Honor."

I said, "Even if the patient history did fall under the hearsay exception—and it doesn't—the best evidence rule excludes this doctor's testimony. There is a written hospital record, which is itself the best evidence of the history given by the patient. In fact, after eight years, it is all but certain that everything this witness knows about the case has come from reviewing that record. The prosecution should use this witness to authenticate the record and admit it into evidence as the best evidence of the patient history."

"I'm entitled to present my case in the manner of my choosing," Maxwell said.

Having said all there was to say, we waited while the judge sucked his colorless lips, looking first at Maxwell, then at me from beneath his bushy eyebrows. "I'm going to allow the question," he said.

It was a blow, a heavy one. I went back to my seat thinking about the possibilities for appeal if we lost at trial, and Maxwell returned to the lectern. The white noise in the courtroom faded.

Maxwell said to Dr. Rosen, "Please give us the history of frostbite given to you by Mr. Hill for purposes of diagnosis and treatment."

"This was eight years ago in early February, February 4. Snow fell for most of the day and into the evening, and the road conditions were bad and getting worse. The temperature never got out of the teens. Mr. Hill and a friend of his went out driving, evidently just to drink beer and slide around. Mr. Hill ingested more than a half-dozen cans of beer. He and his friend were working their way through a case."

"Who was driving, Mr. Hill or his friend?"

"The friend."

This was clearly outside the personal knowledge of the witness, but an objection might serve no purpose other than to emphasize the damaging nature of the testimony. It didn't really matter who was driving.

"What accounted for Mr. Hill's long exposure to the elements?" Maxwell asked. "Did their car get stuck?"

"Mr. Hill needed to urinate. His friend stopped the car, and Mr. Hill got out to relieve himself. While he was doing it, his friend drove off and left him."

"There in the snowstorm."

"Yes. In the snowstorm, at dusk, on a thinly traveled road. It was roughly ninety minutes before Mr. Hill could attract the attention of a motorist, who then transported him to the hospital."

"Who was the friend who left him in the snowstorm that day?"

"A man named Bob Shorter."

Maxwell looked at Shorter, and every eye in the courtroom followed his gaze. Shorter remained expressionless.

"Thank you, Doctor."

It was my turn to cross-examine. "Doctor, did you personally take down the patient's history?"

"In part. The admissions nurse would have begun the history, and I would have edited it after talking to the patient."

"Would have? You don't specifically remember doing so?"

"I have a sense that I did."

"Did the patient say the name Bob Shorter to you, or was it already in the notes?"

"Both, I think. My memory is that he kept saying the name over and over: 'Shorter did this to me.

Shorter left me by the road in a blizzard.' That sort of thing."

"But you have no way of knowing that it was, in fact, Shorter who had done it to him."

"No, just what he told me."

"If Mr. Hill was angry at Bob Shorter, if they had just had a violent argument, or if Shorter had wronged him in some other way, then Mr. Hill might have just been getting back at him."

"Maybe. It didn't strike me that way."

"Or maybe Mr. Hill was trying to account for his presence in the snow without implicating himself in some wrongdoing we don't know anything about."

The witness didn't respond, but of course I hadn't asked him a question. I said, "Did you question him closely about the events of the evening, specifically about whom he'd been with?"

"I doubt it."

"You didn't press him on any of those points."

"Just what I needed for diagnosis and treatment."

"Which wouldn't have included anything about Shorter."

"Well, I remember being interested. It was quite a story. That's why I remember it all these years later."

The testimony wasn't getting any better from my point of view.

"No further questions," I said.

When I sat down, Shorter pushed a paper toward me on which he had written, "You should have been able to keep the jury from hearing that."

I wrote underneath his words, "You should have refrained from evil," and pushed the paper back to him.

Chapter 12

For lunch Brooke and I walked to the Richmond on Broad Café. Ironically, after we'd gotten our food, we sat at the same table where Mike and Sarah had had their rendezvous. It reminded me that I'd promised Mike McMillan a favor. As Brooke took a sip of her water, I got out my phone. Mike had texted me Sarah Fleckman's number. I opened my messages and tapped her name.

"Who are you calling?" Brooke asked as I put the phone to my ear.

She should suspect the answer, I thought, if Mike had told her about finding Sarah in his bed. "Just listen. Don't let your head explode. I'll explain afterward."

A woman answered.

"Hi, Sarah. This is Robin Starling. I'm a lawyer with an office in the Ironfronts on Main." Brooke's chin lowered, her eyes fixed on me.

"I know who you are," Sarah said.

"Oh, good. I know we've met a couple of times." I gave a small laugh. "I really couldn't tell you when or where."

"Really? The first time was at Arts in the Park. You were with John Parker."

That name was a blast from the past.

"I dated John awhile before you did, which is why I noticed you particularly. It was interesting to see who he'd taken up with after me."

Okay, it was coming back to me. She'd been with someone, too, but I couldn't quite bring him into focus.

"I was with another lawyer myself. Mike McMillan."

So I'd met him before the first time I'd run into him with Paul, and I hadn't remembered.

"I understand you're with Paul Soldano now," Sarah said. "How's that going?" The conversation was beginning to feel a bit creepy.

"Good," I said. "Paul's a sweetie."

"Is he. He never had any use for me, I can tell you that. Paul Soldano was not a fan."

"I wonder if we could meet for coffee sometime in the next couple of days."

There was a silence. "I guess," she said. "How come?"

"I'll tell you when I see you, if that's all right. Would tomorrow morning work?"

It wouldn't. We got it settled for the day after that, seven thirty at the Coffee Grounds. It was another bit of irony in that Brooke's brother, Brian, and his girlfriend were the co-owners.

"Okay," Brooke said when I'd hung up. "This I've got to hear."

I sensed a land mine, so I took a big bite of my salad wrap and chewed while I thought about it. "Gotta to be back in court soon," I mumbled through my food by way of excuse, gesturing at my working jaws. I waited until I swallowed before I said anything else. Brooke waited, too, not touching her food.

"Mike asked me to talk to her," I said. "Convince her to leave him alone."

"So what's she done now?"

"Evidently, when she and Mike stopped seeing each other, she returned his key. Just what you'd expect."

"The key to his house?"

I nodded. "But she seems to have made a copy of it first."

Brooke pushed her food away. I put a hand on her tray and pushed it back in front of her. "Eat," I said. "You'll like this. Okay. She let herself into his house while we were all at Enrique's last night. Mike got home, no idea anyone was in the house. He hung up his suit, washed his face, brushed his teeth, pulled on a T-shirt, and climbed into his unmade bed."

"And she was there."

"Wearing nothing but her own skin. Mike came out of the bed like he'd been scalded, went down the stairs and straight out the front door, leaving Sarah in possession of his house. He went to Paul's. Both of them were at my place before midnight." I took another bite of my wrap and chewed. Brooke waited. I gave up and swallowed.

"They went back to Paul's to spend the night. The way we left it, I was going to talk to Sarah."

"Was anyone going to talk to me?"

I moved my head. "I thought Mike was, but maybe I misunderstood. Maybe that was my job, too."

"So talking to me is a job?"

"I didn't mean it that way. I have to say, though—I had no idea how you'd react. He probably didn't, either. My thinking is he's scared to broach the subject of Sarah."

"Scared of me?"

I took another bite of my wrap, and, finally, she pulled over her own tray and started eating.

"I guess I have been a bit touchy on the subject of Sarah," she said finally.

"A bit," I said.

She ate some more. She took a sip of her water, choked, and snorted the water out through her nose. "I'm just picturing Mike's face at the moment he realized he's not alone in the bed," she said in a strangled voice.

"Eyes go wide, heart pounding," I said.

"She says something, and he realizes it's Sarah."

"This limpet that seems to have attached herself to him and won't let go."

"'Came out of bed like he'd been scalded.' I can just picture it."

It wasn't long before we both had the giggles.

"Poor Mike," Brooke said. "Not one scary woman in his life, but two."

"And one's about all any man can handle."

After the lunch break, Maxwell called Valerie Shaw to the witness stand. She had dressed up for the occasion, and her tight dress accented her beefy physique. If Shorter's tombstones were to be believed, Val was forty-eight and had no mate. I knew from personal experience that she had a voice like metal screeching on metal.

"Do I know Bob Shorter!" she exclaimed in response to questions. "Sure I know him! I know Bob Shorter just like I knew Bill Hill. I saw every day how they hated each other."

I doubted the "every day" part. Also, "they hated each other" was an opinion, something only a witness who had been qualified as an expert was entitled to give. Nonexperts were supposed to testify to the facts and let the jury draw its own conclusions. I didn't object, though, because the facts and not Val's opinions were what was going to kill us.

"I'm not asking you about how they felt about each other," Maxwell said with a curious glance in my direction. "Just whether you ever observed any conflict between the two men."

"There was that time Mr. Shorter beat Mr. Hill's dog half to death—is that what you mean?"

Yes, that was what he meant. Of course it was what he meant. Bill's dog had died, Melissa Stimmler had told me, but she had left out some crucial details.

Her purse clutched in front of her, Valerie told the jury that Bob Shorter took long walks through the neighborhood, one or two a day, and he always carried an ax handle with him. "My equalizer," he'd called it on more than one occasion, even though no one ever asked him, not as far as she knew. Anyway, Buster, Mr. Hill's dog, had gotten out, and Mr. Shorter claimed it had attacked him. No one saw Buster attack Bob Shorter, of course. Valerie had seen him hitting Buster, though, not just once but again and again. "He brought that ax handle down," Valerie said, raising her own fist over her head and striking down with it. "Thump! He raised it, and he brought it down again. Thump! I ran out onto my lawn, screaming at him to stop, but he hit that poor, yelping animal another time or two before he did. When Bob Shorter turned to me, his face had a funny yellow color to it, and I thought for a moment he was going to come at *me*. At least I distracted him from that poor dog, though, and it was able to drag itself out of Mr. Shorter's reach. You should have heard him! Buster was whining just as pitiful as anything you could imagine. It never did walk right after that. It just dragged itself around the house, Mr. Hill said. Didn't live too long, either, maybe six months or so, and Mr. Hill had to have it put down. It was just in so much pain, you know?" She had worked herself up to the point that her face was red and tears were beginning to run down her cheeks.

"What did you do after witnessing Bob Shorter beat the dog?"

"I called the police, of course, but nothing came of it. I think there was some kind of plea bargain, and Bob Shorter paid a fine, but he never went to jail or anything."

"No further questions," Maxwell said.

The judge looked at me. "Ms. Starling?"

Every member of the jury was looking at Bob Shorter, each with some expression of revulsion. I myself wanted to do nothing so much as to break off a table leg and beat Shorter to a bloody pulp with it. Instead I got up and went to the lectern.

"Ms. Shaw," I said.

She sniffed loudly and raised her tear-streaked face.

"Ms. Shaw, did you ever see Bob Shorter strike down a little old lady on the street, maybe because she had the gall to wish him good morning?"

"What?" There was a silence in the courtroom. Finally, she said, "No, I never saw him do that."

"As far as you know, has Mr. Shorter ever snatched up a baby and dashed its brains out on the pavement?"

"No! Of course not."

"Of course not?" I walked back to my table and stood behind my client. "You think there's a limit to Bob Shorter's depravity, then?"

"Well, I . . ." She sniffed again, loudly. "I don't know."

"Your Honor," Maxwell said, "Valerie Shaw hasn't been qualified as an expert on the depravity of men."

"I just wanted to save counsel the trouble of presenting more evidence that this man is a monster," I said. "He clearly is just that. If there's such a thing as a demon in human form, then he's sitting right here at this table. You want the jury to believe Bob Shorter hated Bill Hill. Of course he did! He hated everyone. That's not the question before us. The only question before us is whether sometime on March 9, Mr. Shorter walked over to Bill Hill's house, stabbed him where he sat, and left him to bleed out on the floor while he went home to change his clothes before dinner. Would he have had any scruples about doing so? Probably not. Did he do it? There's some evidence that he did, but evidence can be manufactured, and as much as he hated his neighbors, his neighbors hated him. In weighing the evidence—"

"You're arguing your case," Maxwell objected.

It had taken him a long time to get there, probably because he'd been so stunned by the direction my argument had taken. I was a bit stunned myself.

"I have no further questions," I said. I sat beside my client, reflected a moment, then moved my chair about a foot farther away.

Chapter 13

I made the newspaper, front page above the fold. The headline was "Lawyer Says Client a Monster." The newspaper had evidently gotten a transcript from the court reporter, or else had a reporter of its own at the trial taking shorthand, because they got my whole speech word for word, including such memorable phrases as "demon in human form." Dr. McDermott brought his copy of the paper over while I was having my morning bowl of granola with Greek yogurt stirred in. He sat and scratched Deeks's ears while I read the article.

"You're making a name for yourself," he said when I looked up.

"New clients are going to be flocking to my door."

"Are you playing a deep game that's difficult for us laymen to grasp?"

"I'm just conceding the obvious. Shorter's character has been trashed beyond the possibility of rehabilitation. I can exhaust my credibility trying to convince the jury he's a good guy, or I can give up that point and try to focus the jury on the facts of the case. Not even a monster can have committed every crime that's occurred in the city of Richmond."

"Not even a demon in human form?"

"I may have gone a bit overboard there." Deeks gave Dr. McDermott's hand a lick and ran out of the kitchen.

"And this monster is connected to this particular crime by fingerprint and blood evidence," Dr. McDermott said.

"Well, yes."

"If you win this one, you'll have established a reputation as a miracle worker."

I nodded glumly. "Great."

"That would be a good thing, wouldn't it?"

"I guess. Every sleazeball in the city will want me to represent him, but it's work."

"It's not really likely you'll win, though, is it?" Deeks reappeared, and Dr. McDermott took the ball Deeks offered him.

"No," I said. Deeks's eyes were focused on the ball like a missile guidance system.

"What are the consequences of losing?"

"At this point? Suit for malpractice. Disciplinary proceedings."

"So you've got to win."

"If I can."

"You don't sound as pumped up as usual."

"I don't feel as pumped up as usual."

"That's a bummer," Dr. McDermott said.

"It is that," I agreed.

Rodney Burns, the private detective in my office cluster, was also a subscriber to the *Richmond Times-Dispatch*. He was in Brooke's office with a copy of it when I got to work.

"Shouldn't you be in trial?" Brooke asked.

"Doesn't start until ten o'clock this morning. Judge had some motions in other cases to take care of."

"So you're here to plan your strategy for the day?"

"Sort of."

"Sort of?"

"My plan was to sit and think and hope something comes to me."

Brooke's eyes focused on something behind me, and I turned to see Paul coming through the archway of exposed brick. He had a newspaper.

"You don't even subscribe," I said.

"Mike called me. I picked it up on the way over."

"How did you know she'd be here?" Brooke asked. "She's supposed to be in trial."

"She told me last night court was starting late this morning."

"So you knew about this."

"No. She didn't say anything about turning on her client and gutting him like a deer."

"I didn't want to think about it," I said.

"Shouldn't you say, 'Gutting him like a monster'?" Rodney Burns asked.

"Or 'Gutting him like a demon in human form'?" Brooke said.

"I take it you've given up on the case," Paul said.

"No, I've just repositioned myself. Think of it as a strategic retreat."

"Is it strategic to jump down a well?"

"I don't get it," Brooke said. "Jump down a well?"

"He's probably got some kind of Civil War image in mind," I said. "Analogies aren't really Paul's strong suit."

Mike McMillan came in. He, too, had a paper. We shifted to make room for him in Brooke's small office. "I need to get more chairs," she said, looking apologetically at Mike.

"You've got enough," Rodney said. "What with chairs, desk, table, file cabinet, everybody's got a place to perch."

Mike kissed Brooke's cheek, which seemed to irritate rather than please her, and parked his hip on the file cabinet. He looked at me. "What were you thinking? I don't do a lot of trial work, but I have to say, I don't get it."

"It's a strategic retreat," Brooke said. "She's maneuvering the prosecution to just where she wants him."

"Really? There's a plan?"

I exhaled. "No, not really. I had two choices: try to expose Valerie Shaw as a liar or do something really desperate."

"I can see you chose desperate," Mike said. "Does that mean you don't think she was lying?"

"No, I don't. I don't think I'd have accomplished anything if I'd gone that route. I'd have just damaged my credibility."

"And as it is? Do you think you did your case some good?"

"I don't know. I confess, I wasn't following any grand strategy. I got caught up in the moment."

"Mike's worried," Paul said. "He thinks you could lose your law license over this."

"And thirty thousand dollars isn't nearly compensation enough for this case if you lose your license," Mike said. "Have you looked at the rules of professional conduct recently?"

"I think I read an article in the *Virginia Bar Journal* a couple of months ago," I said. "I took a course in law school."

"A lawyer shall not intentionally prejudice or damage a client during the course of the professional relationship," Mike said. "That's pretty much a quote. Your client files a complaint against you with the state bar, and the disciplinary committee is not going to be kind. Heck, he may not even have to file a complaint. It's on the front page of the paper. The disciplinary committee may take it up on its own, especially since they're already looking into your intimidation of witnesses."

"My alleged intimidation," I corrected. "Of a single witness. And as for yesterday, if I win the case, the committee will have a hard time arguing I damaged my client."

"What are your chances of that?"

I didn't say anything.

"Somewhere between slim and none," Paul said for me.

"I think you're overstating her chances," Mike told him.

There were too many people in the office for me to focus on the upcoming day in court, so I left for the courthouse early. When I got there, the courtroom was virtually empty, Judge Cooley evidently having disposed of his early-morning motions.

Unfortunately, I still didn't have a grand plan to work on. I opened my briefcase and got out my photograph folders: police photographs of the crime scene, police photographs from Bob Shorter's house, the photographs Brooke and I had taken. I flipped through them as spectators and court personnel drifted into the courtroom. When a deputy sheriff brought in my client, I was staring at a photograph of Bill Hill's medicine cabinet.

Shorter dropped into the seat next to me as Ian Maxwell pushed through the bar. "If it isn't my backstabbing lawyer," Shorter said to me. "What are you working on?"

If it isn't my devil in the dock, I thought. The dock was the enclosed space where the accused used to stand in British courtrooms. We didn't have such enclosed spaces for prisoners in US courtrooms, but the expression persisted. "I was just thinking Bill Hill took a lot pills," I said.

"He was a hypochondriac, like I told you."

I glanced over at the prosecution's table, where Ian Maxwell was arranging folders and legal pads. The bailiff strode to the front of the courtroom and demanded we all rise. We stood as he called the court into session, and Judge Cooley entered, stopping and blinking at us as if surprised to find his courtroom full of people.

Maxwell's first witness of the day was Jerry Patterson, who lived across the street from Shorter. "I've lived in the same house for twenty-four years," he said. He looked to be in his seventies, with liver spots on his face and thin, white hair parted on one side. "I knew

Bill back when he still had both his feet. He and Bob Shorter used to be pretty close. They came and went through the alley that runs along the side of my house. The two of 'em, Bill and Bob, would sit out on Bill's patio back of his house and drink beer. Last four or five years I seen Bill sitting on his patio alone sometimes, but he don't go over to Bob Shorter's no more, and Bob Shorter don't go to his place. Tell the truth, I seen Bill in his backyard less and less as the years passed. Mostly he'd be a-sitting in his living room, staring out the picture window and watching the world go by. I seen him there when I drove out for groceries or to go to my lodge meetings."

"Would he wave to you when you passed him?" Maxwell asked.

"Yeah, sometimes. I tell you one person he didn't never wave to, though, and that was Bob Shorter. He'd fix his gaze on Bob as Bob went by the house on his walks, and Bill's face would tighten, and he'd keep his eyes locked on Bob until he disappeared down the street. Between you and me and the fence post, I think Bob Shorter did it on purpose. He walked past Bill's house pretty much every time he went out, just to be sure Bill could see him walking around on his healthy legs and feet."

Maxwell glanced at me. I could have objected to this obvious introduction of the witness's opinion, maybe asked whether he based this opinion on anything Shorter had said or whether he had it from the fence post on good authority, but I didn't see anything to be gained from beating up on Shorter's neighbors. Maxwell asked, "Do you recall any occasion in particular?"

"Well. I was driving home one day when I seen Bob Shorter across the street from Bill's house, a-pointin' his stick at Bill there in the window, Bill starin' back at him. You know about Bob's equalizer, don't you?"

Maxwell's mouth quirked. "We've heard about it, yes."

"People are kinda leery of old Bob and his equalizer, myself included."

Matthew Quinn testified next. He was a younger guy, maybe early thirties, who worked as a nurse at Saint Mary's. He lived two streets over from Bill Hill and Bob Shorter and from his property didn't have a line of sight to either of their houses. "Then how do you know the defendant, Bob Shorter?" Maxwell asked him.

"I run in the same neighborhood where Mr. Shorter takes his walks." Matthew's dark hair was neatly trimmed, and he wore khakis and a green sweater over a white dress shirt.

"How often do you encounter Bob Shorter?"

Mathew smiled. "Less than I used to. I make an effort to avoid him."

"Why is that?"

"I nodded to him once as I went by him on the street, and he lunged at me with that stick he carries."

"Why did he do that?"

Matthew shook his head. "Maybe he thought I was passing too close to him. I was five or six miles into my run, pretty sweaty, and I may not have smelled too fresh. Anyway, he lunged at me, and when I jumped away from him, I tripped on the curb

168

and fell onto someone's lawn. I got maybe a dozen grass burrs in one forearm that I had to pick out afterwards."

"So you avoided him after that? Turned down another street when you saw him coming, crossed to the other side of the street, that sort of thing?"

"Yes. And when I started running with my little girl—I have a twelve-month-old and push her sometimes in a running stroller—I got a gun."

"You got a gun," Maxwell repeated.

"Just a little derringer I carry in a pocket holster. I feel better with it there. I mean, suppose he knocked me down one day and went after my little Emily?"

My gaze slid to Shorter. His eyes were on Matthew, his lip curled with an expression I took as a look of disdain. I stood up. "Your Honor, may we approach the bench?"

Judge Cooley nodded. Maxwell and I went forward, and the white noise went up.

"Your Honor," I said. "I think this testimony might be grounds for a mistrial. It has nothing to do with the relationship between the defendant and Bill Hill, and nothing to do with the murder weapon. We don't even know when this so-called lunge occurred in relation to the time of the murder."

"I'm coming to that," Maxwell said.

"This testimony is not probative at all, and it's highly prejudicial. I don't think the prejudice can be cured by striking the testimony and admonishing the jury. The jury's heard it, and it can't unhear it."

"Bob Shorter's neighbors were scared of him, afraid of actual physical violence. That's relevant, Your Honor."

"You can't convict a man of murder because he's a scary guy," I said.

"I'm going to strike it," Judge Cooley said, "and I'll admonish the jury not to consider it in their deliberations." He eyed me over the half lenses of his glasses. "I'm not going to declare a mistrial. If it comes to it, no doubt you'll do what you can with it on appeal."

I nodded my head in acceptance. I'd never expected a mistrial. Getting the testimony stricken was going to increase my credibility with the jury and diminish Maxwell's, though.

The judge struck the testimony, admonished the jury, and recessed for lunch.

"You need to watch your facial expressions," I told Shorter as the jury filed out. "You can't sit there sneering at the witnesses. The jury already doesn't like you. Don't give them anything else to work with."

"What am I supposed to do? Just smile and pretend to enjoy this parade of assholes trying to railroad me into the gas chamber?"

"Into death by lethal injection," I corrected. "Or the electric chair, if you prefer it. Virginia doesn't use the gas chamber. Look, I know you hate everyone. Fine, but you can't show it. Wear an expression of concern. Try to look surprised now and then that actions of yours that were so entirely innocent could have been misconstrued by whoever it is that's testifying."

"You want me to be an actor."

"Exactly. You're a nice old man who got off on the wrong foot with his neighbors. All you want is a chance to explain yourself, to heal the breaches in all these relationships."

He rolled his eyes as he stood for the sheriff's deputy to cuff him. "Do you really think . . ." He broke off. "Ah, hell. I'll do what I can."

Chapter 14

After lunch, a sheriff's deputy brought in Bob Shorter and uncuffed him so he could take a seat. As you may have noticed, the ritual of cuffing and uncuffing always takes place while the jury is out of the courtroom. Seeing a man in shackles a couple of times a day is likely to prejudice a jury of his peers.

I sat silently beside my client as the courtroom filled behind us. This time I wasn't looking through photographs or flipping through my notes. I was just sitting. Eventually I glanced at my watch. Maxwell was late.

Shorter leaned toward me. "You know why nobody likes me, don't you?"

I rolled my head toward him and raised my eyebrows.

"It's not because I carry an ax handle or that I look at people the wrong way. It's because they can't control me."

"I thought it was because you were a nasty piece of work."

"Come on, Starling. You're better than that. Social conventions, religion, law . . . all of it is designed to control us, to bend us to the will of others. We reject that. We can be independent, free, completely autonomous."

I glanced behind me, but no one seemed to be within earshot. "Are you telling me you killed Bill Hill?"

"No. You're missing the point."

"You're saying you could have killed him and felt no moral compunctions about doing it."

"Well, yes. I didn't, though. I told you I didn't."

"Yes, you told me. I'm thinking we've been indoctrinated to tell the truth, though. That it's one more attempt by society to control us. It doesn't work with you, though, does it?"

"You don't like me, do you?"

"Should I? If you want me to like you, then I'm controlling you. If I ought to like you, then you're controlling me. Enlightened people such as ourselves reject that."

Maxwell pushed through the rail. This time Aubrey Biggs, Richmond's vertically challenged commonwealth's attorney, was with him. Biggs met my gaze and smiled, an expression that made him look like the Grinch as he contemplated the evils he was planning to inflict on Whoville.

"Who's that?" Shorter asked, and my skin prickled at the feel of his breath on my shoulder and the smell of cigarette smoke.

"Richmond's commonwealth attorney," I said.

"Moving in for the kill?"

"Maybe. He may have the idea I'm self-destructing, and he just wants to watch."

"Wonder what gave him the idea you're self-destructing."

The jury started coming in. "Remember what I told you," I said. "Your performance starts now."

Once again the bailiff called the court to order. When everyone sat, Aubrey Biggs remained on his feet. Judge Cooley's eyes fixed on him. "Mr. Biggs? To what do we owe the pleasure?"

"If it please the court, I'm joining Mr. Maxwell as 'of counsel' in this case."

The judge's mouth worked. "I can't say that it does please me particularly, but if you must, you must."

Someone in the jury laughed. My gaze focused on a skinny young man in a three-piece suit and several days' growth of beard. He was still grinning, and the light from the overhead fluorescents winked from one lens of his glasses. I got my jury folder out of my briefcase and flipped it open. The juror was Andrew Hartman, age twenty-nine, logistics analyst with WestRock.

Biggs himself went to the lectern to call the prosecution's next witness: Larkin Entwistle. Biggs had cleaned him up for the occasion. Larkin came to the stand wearing khakis and polished loafers rather than the baggy jeans stuffed into oversize, unlaced high-tops I'd last seen him in. His long bangs were combed back off his face, and his shirt was a white button-down. Overall he looked like someone a girl could take home to meet her parents.

As Larkin was swearing to tell the truth, the whole truth, and nothing but the truth, I glanced at Maxwell, seated alone at the prosecution's table. He gave me a shrug. Larkin stepped up into the witness box and took a seat, slouching and looking at Biggs through slitted eyes. *Hard to take the 'hood out of the boy,*

I thought. Biggs moved from behind the lectern to stand next to it, honoring an adage of good showmanship: show them your body.

"Mr. Entwistle," he said. "Could you tell us your full name?"

Larkin nodded. "Larkin Entwistle."

"How old are you, Mr. Entwistle?"

"You can call me Larkin. Mr. Entwistle's my old man."

Biggs gave him a smile and a nod. "Larkin. Very well. How old are you, Larkin?"

"Seventeen."

"Have you ever been in a courtroom before?"

Larkin shook his head.

"Witness indicates no," Biggs said. To Larkin he said, "It's not such a scary place, is it? I ask questions—you answer them. When we're done, Ms. Robin Starling, the attorney for the defense, will ask you some questions. That's all it is: question and answer, question and answer. We're having a conversation."

Larkin continued to sit with his head back, looking at Biggs from beneath lowered eyelids. If Biggs relaxed him any more, he was going to slide out of his chair.

Biggs smoothed his jacket against his sides. "What can you tell us about the events of Friday, March 9?" he asked Larkin. "Do you remember March 9?"

"Sure. It was the day old Mr. Shorter offed Bill Hill."

There was a stir in the gallery and among the jurors, and Biggs looked at the judge. "We'll strike the last part of Mr. Entwistle's answer."

Judge Cooley nodded. To the jury he said, "The witness has just offered an answer to the ultimate question, which it is incumbent on you to decide. You're to disregard it."

"Did you see Mr. Shorter that day?" Biggs asked Larkin.

"Sure did. I seen him coming out of Hill's place."

"That's the house owned by William Hill, the decedent?"

"That would be the one."

"And the man you saw coming out of that house was the defendant in this case, the man seated right there in this courtroom." He pointed, and Larkin nodded.

Biggs said, "Your responses to my questions need to be oral so the court reporter can get them down. Can you do that for us?"

Larkin nodded again. "I got it. My response is oral. Right."

"Very well. What time was it when you saw the defendant Robert Shorter coming out of William Hill's house?"

"Oral," Larkin said.

In the jury box, Andrew Hartman's bray of laughter was immediate. Others in the courtroom were a bit slower on the uptake, but the laughter grew until Judge Cooley quelled it with a few bangs of his gavel.

"That's enough," the judge told the courtroom. He looked over the tops of his glasses at Larkin.

"Young man," he said, and he waited until Larkin looked up at him. "I see you have a sense of humor. Very good, but this is not the place for it."

"Sorry, Judge."

"You may call me 'Your Honor.'"

Larkin gave a nod. "Sorry, Your Honor. He just set it up so nice, you know?"

Judge Cooley's mouth stretched, but it was more an expression of distaste than a smile. "Just respond to the questions out loud rather than with head shakes and nods. Do you understand?"

Larkin nodded.

"Out loud, Mr. Larkin."

"I can do that."

With a glance at the jury box, Biggs asked again, "What time did you see Robert Shorter coming out of William Hill's house?"

"It musta been four o'clock or maybe a little before. I'd just got back from school."

"That's the Armstrong High School?"

Larkin started to nod, stopped himself, and said, "Yes. Armstrong High School."

"Do you take the bus to and from school?"

"Every day."

"Where is the bus stop in relation to William Hill's house?"

"Down the street maybe half a block."

"You got off the bus and were walking home when you saw Robert Shorter?"

"That's right."

"Could you describe him for us?"

"He looked just like that old man sitting right there." Larkin pointed at Shorter.

Another wave of laughter swept the courtroom, and this time the judge didn't try to stop it. Biggs, getting red in the face, took a breath and exhaled it slowly as the laughter faded.

"Did he look just like he looks now? Was he wearing the same clothes, for instance?"

"Oh, do you mean was he covered with blood?"

"Was he?"

"Yeah, he had blood on him, on his pants and one sleeve of his shirt, I think."

"Where did you see him in relation to William Hill's house?"

"Coming out, like I said. He come out, and he walked to the street and turned toward his own house."

"Was he carrying anything? Anything in his hands?"

"Just that old ax handle he always carries."

Biggs looked at me, then back at the witness. "Have you ever had occasion to talk to Ms. Starling, the defendant's attorney?"

"Sure."

"Tell us about that occasion, please."

"I told her just what I'm telling you about seeing Mr. Shorter." Larkin moistened his lips with his tongue. "She told me not to tell anyone."

"Counsel for the defense said this? Not to tell anyone?"

Larkin nodded. "Don't tell anyone or else."

"She said, 'Or else'? Or else what?"

Larkin shrugged. "Or else nothing."

"She didn't threaten you more specifically?"

I stood. "Objection. Counsel is leading the witness."

Biggs looked at me as if I were a species of vermin.

"Sustained," Judge Cooley said.

Larkin said, "Oh, you mean like with the ax handle?"

"Did she threaten you with an ax handle?" Biggs asked.

"Sure did." Emphatic nod. "She had old Mr. Shorter's equalizer that day, and she was waving it around like a crazy woman, knocking everybody down and stuff. 'You talk to the police, and I be bustin' some heads,' she said. 'You talk to *anyone* about this, and I be bustin' heads.'"

Biggs went to his table and extracted some eight-by-ten photographs from a folder. He held them up. "May I?" he asked the judge.

Cooley nodded his assent, and Biggs brought one of the photographs to my table and took another to the judge. The third photograph he held out to the witness. As I looked at my own copy, which showed me standing over Larkin's friend Warren with the ax handle, I smelled Shorter's tobacco breath and felt him looking over my shoulder. I didn't look at him.

Biggs said, "Can you identify this photograph?"

"Sure can. It's a picture of Mr. Shorter's lawyer there beating my friend Warren with that ax handle I told you about."

"Objection," I said, half standing and trying to sound bored. "Relevance."

"Does the photograph fairly represent what was happening on the occasion of your meeting with Ms. Starling?" Biggs asked his witness.

"Your Honor, that question is misconduct," I said. "He is trying to get this testimony before the jury without giving the court the opportunity to rule on my objection."

The judge held his hand toward Larkin Entwistle, his palm out, but he was looking at me. "Approach the bench, both of you."

We went forward and stood looking up. The court reporter moved closer, as well, pushing the bench-conference button to trigger the white noise.

"Mr. Biggs, what is the relevance of this photograph?"

"It shows that the defendant has been trying, through his attorney, to suppress evidence against him."

"That would be a very serious matter, and certainly relevant to these proceedings," Judge Cooley told me.

"It would be if it were true, but Mr. Biggs has presented no evidence that Bob Shorter orchestrated the events the witness has just related or that he even knew about them before this moment."

"It may well show that counsel has made herself an accessory after the fact to the crime of murder," Biggs said.

"I am not on trial."

"Yet," Biggs said.

"I am not on trial yet," I amended. "When I am, we can come back to the question of the relevance of this photograph."

Judge Cooley fixed his gaze on Biggs. "Do you have evidence linking the defendant to these events, Mr. Big?"

"Biggs, Your Honor. No. Not at this time."

"Then this line of inquiry is over," Judge Cooley said.

"Thank you, Your Honor," I said.

The judge gave me a baleful look, but Biggs was more entertaining. His neck swelled up, his face reddened, and his nostrils flared.

"Do you understand me, Mr. Big?" Judge Cooley said.

"Biggs, Your Honor. I understand you." Despite the circumstances, I felt a surge of something very like joy. It was moments like this that made me love trial work.

"Very well." Judge Cooley nodded to the court reporter, who turned off the white noise and moved back to his seat near the witness stand.

"Mr. Big, you may continue."

"No further questions, Your Honor." He looked at me, and his mouth twisted as if he smelled something sour. "Your witness."

"Thank you, Mr. Bigness." Feeling unaccountably lighthearted, I went to the lectern. "Hi, Larkin."

Larkin smirked at me.

"I guess the last time I saw you was when I found you and your friends all over the hood of my car. You and Warren and . . . who was your other buddy?"

Biggs sprang to his feet. "Your Honor, the court has ruled this line of inquiry irrelevant. To proceed with it in light of that ruling is misconduct."

Judge Cooley looked at me over the top of his glasses, fixing me with his gaze. "Counsel would seem to have a point, Ms. Sterling."

I was enjoying myself too much to correct the mispronunciation of my name. "Could we ask the court reporter to read back the last question Mr. Biggs asked his witness, along with the response to that question?"

The judge looked at his court reporter. "Mr. Yielding?

Mr. Yielding, a middle-aged man with thick, iron-gray hair, peered at the display of his paperless stenograph machine as he scrolled back through the testimony. He said, "Mr. Biggs: Can you identify this photograph? Witness: Sure can. It's a picture of Mr. Shorter's lawyer there beating my friend Warren with that ax handle I told you about."

"That's in the record on direct," I said. "Since Mr. Biggs elicited testimony about one part of the encounter, I'm entitled to go into all of it on cross-examination."

"Your Honor, that testimony was stricken from the record."

I smiled. "I don't believe it was. The judge ruled that your photograph was irrelevant, but that inflammatory bit of testimony is still in the record."

"I move that it be stricken," Biggs said.

"And I oppose that motion, Your Honor. The jury heard the testimony, and once heard it can't be unheard. I need to be allowed to cross-examine."

"The court can admonish the jury," Biggs said.

"An admonishment is not going to make the jury unhear the inflammatory but irrelevant testimony that you have just elicited."

"If it's irrelevant, it's irrelevant. If the testimony isn't probative of any issue in the case, there's nothing to correct."

"Testimony can be prejudicial without being probative," I said. "That's the very sort of testimony that requires correction." I looked up the judge. "Further cross-examination is within the discretion of the court, Your Honor. I will abide by your ruling." It was hardly a concession. I had no choice but to abide by the court's ruling, but I was doing what I could to appear meek and reasonable.

The judge tapped his bench with his pen. I actually thought that this was an argument I ought to lose, but there's an old story about an elderly trial lawyer at his retirement dinner. In his speech, he said, "When I was young and inexperienced, I lost many cases I should have won. When I was older and more experienced, I won many cases I should have lost. So on the whole, I'd have to say that justice was done."

"I'm going to allow a few questions along this line," the judge said. "Objection overruled." If it were me, I would have cut me off and stricken the offending testimony from the record, but Judge Cooley's ruling was an example of why lawyers tend to make every argument they can think of that is remotely plausible: judges don't always rule the way you think they should.

"Your Honor," Biggs objected.

"The questions may open the door for you to explore this encounter yourself on redirect," Judge Cooley told him.

Biggs hesitated, then nodded.

"Could Mr. Yielding read back my last question?" I asked.

The judge nodded, and Mr. Yielding read, "Ms. Starling: I guess the last time I saw you was when I found you and your friends all over the hood of my car. You and Warren and who was your other buddy."

To the witness I said, "Answer the question, please."

"Nate. Nathan. Nathan Diaz. But we weren't all over the hood of your car."

"No? Perhaps I have something that will refresh your memory." I went to my table and extracted three copies of the photograph that showed Warren and Nathan sitting on my car and Larkin leaning against it. The soles of Nathan's feet were holding him in place high up on the hood, and doubtless it was he who had scratched my red paint.

I delivered copies of the photograph to Biggs and the judge and took the last one to the witness. "Care to tell us what you're looking at, Larkin?"

His lip curled.

"It's a photograph of Warren and Nathan Diaz sitting on the hood of my car, isn't it? And you leaning against it."

"Objection. Relevance," Biggs said, standing.

"It goes to the credibility of the witness," I said. "If he's lying about this, he may be lying about everything he's told us."

"Where did you get this?" Larkin asked. "Did old lady Stimmler give it to you?"

We all turned to look at him. "How did you get the photograph of me with the ax handle, Larkin?" I asked. "Did you force your way into Melissa Stimmler's house and take her phone from her by force and text the photo to yourself?"

He drew his chin in. "She give it to me."

"Does this photograph, the one you're holding now, show your friends sitting on the hood of my car and you leaning against it? Does it?"

He shrugged.

"Oral, Mr. Entwistle."

His lip curled. "Oral," he said.

Someone in the jury box laughed. I didn't look away from the witness, but I'd have put money on it being Andrew Hartman. The judge cut it off with a bang of his gavel.

"This is no place for levity, Ms. Sterling," he told me, though I thought I might have detected a hint of amusement in his gaze. You never know about judges.

"Sorry, Your Honor," I said.

"Young man."

Larkin looked at the judge.

"Does that photograph show your friends sitting on the hood of Ms. Starlet's car, or does it not?"

"I guess."

"Yes or no, Mr. Larkin."

"Yes."

"Does it show you leaning against the car?"

"Yes."

"Yes, Your Honor."

"Your Honor," Larkin said.

"Do you know what perjury is?"

"Yes."

"Has the prosecution shared with you the penalties for it?"

Larkin shrugged.

"It's a class-five felony," Judge Cooley said. "Punishable by a prison sentence of one to ten years or, alternatively, up to twelve months in jail and a fine of not more than two thousand five hundred dollars."

Biggs stood. "Your Honor . . ."

Judge Cooley turned an unfriendly gaze on him. "Yes, Mr. Biggers?"

Biggs winced. "Your Honor, with all due respect, a required element of perjury is that the false testimony be material to the issue being tried. The question of whether Mr. Entwistle was sitting on Ms. Starling's car does not meet that standard."

"Perhaps you can make that point in his trial, Mr. Biggerstaff. Right now I want it understood that I will not tolerate false statements made under oath in my courtroom." He turned back to Larkin, looming over him from the bench. "Is that understood, young man?"

"Yes, sir."

"Yes, Your Honor," the judge corrected. He was an old man, but he could still speak with thunder in his tone.

Larkin swallowed. "Yes, Your Honor."

The judge said, "You claim to have seen Mr. Shorter leaving the decedent's house on March 9. That statement *is* material to the issue being tried. Do you wish to retract that statement?"

186

Larkin's tongue ran along his upper lip, and his gaze went out to the courtroom, where Jenn, his mother, was sitting. "No," he said in a rough voice. He cleared his throat and tried again. "No."

"Very well. Counselor." The judge nodded sharply to me.

I said, "Based on this incident that began with you and your buddies sitting on my car, you filed a complaint against me with the Virginia State Bar. Isn't that correct?"

"Yes."

"Your Honor," Biggs objected. "This is hardly the forum for addressing disciplinary charges against counsel for the defense."

"Then you shouldn't have introduced the matter. Proceed, Ms. Starbuck."

That was really too much. He might as well call me Ms. Startlepuss and be done with it, but I let it go. To Larkin, I said, "Did you file your complaint after talking to Aubrey Biggs, the commonwealth's attorney?"

"Yeah."

"Did Mr. Biggs encourage you to file the complaint?"

Larkin looked at Biggs. "He mentioned it."

"Did he help you draft it?"

"He helped me with some of the words."

Judge Cooley cleared his throat. He'd given me some leeway, but it was time to move on.

"Back to March 9, the day you say you saw Bob Shorter leaving the house of Bill Hill. Are you going to stick with that testimony?"

His tongue brushed his upper lip again. "Yeah, I saw him," he said finally.

"I believe you told Mr. Biggs he was covered in blood?"

"Not covered. He had it on his pants and shirt."

"I think you said the sleeve of his shirt."

"Yeah, on the sleeve."

"Have you seen pictures of the bloody clothes that were found in the residence of Mr. Shorter?"

His eyes again cut to Biggs.

"Mr. Biggs showed you those pictures, didn't he?"

"No."

"No?"

"I didn't see no pictures."

"You didn't see no pictures," I repeated.

"Nah."

"You didn't see the pictures. You saw the clothes themselves—didn't you? Mr. Biggs showed you the bloody clothes."

He shrugged.

"Out loud, Larkin. He showed you the clothes—isn't that right?"

"He gimme a peek at them."

"And you saw the blood on the pants and the sleeve of the shirt."

"I guess."

I turned and looked at Aubrey Biggs, my elbow on the lectern. His face had reddened.

"Well, Larkin," I said, my eyes still on Biggs. "It's easy to see how you managed to describe the condition of the clothes so precisely."

"That's not a question," Biggs said.

"No, it isn't, is it?" I turned back to Larkin. "You say you'd just gotten back from school when you saw Mr. Shorter. Do you mean you were on the way home from school?"

"Yeah, home from the bus stop."

"Your friend Nate walks home with you, doesn't he? Warren's house is in another direction, but Nate and you walk together."

"Nate wasn't with me."

"He didn't go to school that day? He does get off at your bus stop, doesn't he?"

"Yeah, he . . . I think maybe he went home with Warren. I don't remember. He wasn't with me."

"And if I call him to the stand, and he swears to tell the truth under penalty of perjury, he'll tell us the same thing," I said.

"I don't know. How am I supposed to know what he'll say?"

"He might tell us the truth."

Larkin didn't say anything.

"You pass by Melissa Stimmler's house on the way home, don't you? Mr. Hill's next-door neighbor? Do you think she saw you and Nate together that afternoon?"

Light gleamed from a line of sweat that broke free of his hairline to run down his forehead.

"Do we really need to continue with this, Larkin?"

He shook his head.

"Nathan was with you that day, wasn't he?"

Larkin didn't answer, just sat with his head cocked back, and we could hear him breathing.

"I have no further questions of this witness, your honor. But Larkin . . ." I turned back toward him, and he froze, already halfway out of his seat. "If I learn you've bothered Melissa Stimmler for giving me that photograph, harassed her in any way . . ."

"This is outrageous," came a voice from the gallery, interrupting me. Jenn Entwistle was on her feet.

"Your Honor," Biggs objected. "Counsel is threatening the witness right here in open court."

Judge Cooley stood. I'd never seen a judge stand to address counsel before.

"Mr. Biggs." He got the name right, even overarticulated it. He waited.

"Yes, Your Honor?"

"If you don't want to spend the night in jail for contempt of court, you will leave my courtroom now."

"But—"

The judge raised a hand to silence him. "Bailiff!" There was not the hint of a quaver in the word.

Biggs hesitated, then turned abruptly, pushing through the rail and walking down the aisle through the gallery of spectators. He pushed at the big double doors, and when he passed through, they swung shut behind him.

Larkin, who'd been frozen in an awkward crouch half-in and half-out of the witness chair, got his feet under him and began moving toward the rail.

"Bailiff, stop that young man."

Larkin stopped, and the bailiff moved to stand beside him.

"Mr. Max . . . whatever your name is. Mr. Prosecutor. Do you plan to file charges against this miscreant, or do I need to jail him for contempt?"

"I . . . I plan to prosecute," Maxwell said.

The judge took a deep breath and let it out. "Very well." He jerked his head at the bailiff. "Take him away."

The bailiff exited with Larkin through a side door, and the judge fixed his gaze on the jury, moving his gaze from face to face. "Ladies and gentlemen of the jury. Do you need me to tell you what the testimony we've just heard is worth?"

"No," said a voice. It was Andrew Hartman's. "No, you don't."

The judge nodded. He took his seat and picked up his gavel. "Court is in recess until tomorrow morning at nine o'clock." He let his gavel fall, then got up again and left the courtroom through the door behind his bench. After that, it seemed that everyone was talking at once.

I blew out a lungful of air through puffed cheeks and picked my legal pad up off the lectern. Shorter stood as I approached the table and extended a hand. I glanced at the jury, then took it. If Bob Shorter could act a part, then so could I.

Chapter 15

I walked over to Dr. McDermott's house that evening to pick up Deeks as usual. Both dog and old man seemed glad to see me, though Dr. McDermott didn't appear about to wriggle out of his skin. I squatted to rub Deeks's ears, holding his head to avoid a tongue bath. I lost my grip, though, when he surged toward me and fell back on my keister, and Deeks got past my defenses with a cold nose and a warm wet tongue that left a trail of slobber from chin to eyebrows.

"Deeks!" I said in exasperation.

He surged forward again and knocked me onto my back. My dress seemed both tighter and shorter now that I had to wrestle a forty- to fifty-pound puppy just to roll to my hands and knees. Next time I'd change my clothes before walking over.

"How'd you do in court today?" Dr. McDermott asked me as I got to my feet.

"Better than I'm doing picking up my dog, fortunately." I smoothed my skirt.

He smiled. "All I needed was a bag of popcorn."

I gave him a look. Surely he was too old for that to be a lecherous remark.

He cleared his throat. "So, the trial's going better?"

"It went well enough, but the day ended in another explosion. Fortunately, this time it wasn't me who got blown up."

It piqued his interest enough for him to urge me toward the kitchen, where Deeks was audibly slurping water. "I've got a bottle of Riesling in the fridge and a pitcher of tea."

"Riesling."

We sat at the table for me to recount the day in court, and Deeks settled on the floor by my chair with his head resting on my foot. When I got to Judge Cooley's ejection of the commonwealth's attorney from the courtroom, I said, "You should have seen him, standing in his black robes, his voice as hard and sharp as anything I've ever heard. Up to that point in the trial, he was an old man who couldn't get anybody's name right. Then he rose up, a veritable icon of justice. I got goose bumps."

"It sounds like you may pull this one out."

"Hah. It was Judge Cooley's moment of greatness, not mine. I've got a long way to go to reasonable doubt."

"You yourself had a lot to do with what happened today, sounds to me like."

"I've got fingerprint and blood evidence to deal with and a client who brings unity to the masses in their hatred of him."

"My money's on you—or would be, if I could find anyone to bet me."

"Well, thank you."

"You haven't lost a case yet."

"Not a criminal case." I gave him a smile. "I've never died, either. Do you think that means I'm immortal?"

"I don't know. Sometimes I can't help thinking of you as a force of nature."

He smiled, and Deeks gave my ankle a lick. I leaned over to scratch the top of his head—Deeks's head, not Dr. McDermott's.

"I've got nothing on Deeks in the force-of-nature department," I said.

Mike called while I was making dinner—which is to say I had dumped salad from a bag into a bowl and was tearing up deli turkey on it.

"Mike," I said. "What's up?"

"Brooke says you're going to talk to Sarah tomorrow."

"Yep."

"Let me know how it goes, okay?"

"Will do."

There was a pause. "Brooke's thinking you and Paul might like to meet for dinner or something."

"Not tonight. I've already started dinner, and I've got some thinking to do."

"About the case? I'd be willing to serve as a sounding board."

"Maybe tomorrow. Tonight I need to be alone."

I ate my salad. I fed Deeks. I brooded about the case, mentally replaying bits of the recent courtroom action, thinking about what was coming. I got some of my best ideas walking with Deeks, but that night I had one as I was getting a jacket out of the front closet.

I stopped with my hand on the doorknob, Deeks's eyes on my hand.

"Want to go for a ride?" I asked him.

For a moment he didn't move, then he spun and disappeared into the house. In the kitchen I paused to hoist my briefcase to the top of the counter to get out a pen and a blank subpoena. Deeks, already sitting at the door to the garage, gave me a glance, then returned his gaze to the doorknob, his thick tail sweeping the floor.

"I'll take that as a 'Yes, Robin, I do want to go for a ride,'" I said over my shoulder.

As I opened the door, he came up off his front paws in an eager bounce and then was through it. The garage door began to rumble up, but he paid no attention. I opened my car door, and he leaped into my seat, then over the console. He sat looking through the front windshield as if there were something to see—there wasn't, just a paneled wall with a light switch and the controls to the garage door.

I got into the car, and he gave the side of my face a lick. "Oh, come on. We go for rides all the time," I said. "Remember going to Mike's house?" *Remember the hot tub?* I might have said but didn't. It would have been unkind to bring up unpleasant memories.

Deeks turned around on the seat and sat down again.

"You and I are living large," I said, and I turned and backed out of the garage.

Shorter lived on the east side of town. I stroked
Deeks's fur absently as we rode, and he nosed
occasionally at the passenger window. When he
emitted a brief whine I gave in and opened the
window a crack. He put his nose to the opening and
breathed in the crisp, clean air of freedom. After we'd
been on I-64 awhile, he started getting agitated again,
and I unrolled the window enough for him to stick
his head out.

"You're not much of a conversationalist," I said
into the sound of the wind and the road noise.

His tail moved as much as the back of the seat
would let it.

"Ah, the sweet scent of heaven," I said.

The drive to Shorter's neighborhood took
twenty-five minutes, and by the time we got there it
was starting to get dark. When I pulled up at the curb
a block away from Shorter's house, it occurred to me
yet again that I should have brought a leash. I sat
looking at Deeks, and he looked at me, encouraging
me with little moves of his head to open the car door
so we could get out.

"Can you heel?" I asked him.

He bobbed his head, which could have been a
yes, but I was doubtful.

"See, what I'm worried about is protecting you
from Larkin and company if they show up to harass
us," I said. "You'd go right up to them like they were
our best friends in the world."

His eyes on mine, he gave another little whine,
and I sighed. I wished there was a place to park my
car out of sight, but there was only the street. It
wasn't a fanfare of trumpets, but as a calling card my

red bug was pretty unmistakable, even in the deepening twilight. Still, I hoped that since I wasn't leaving it parked in front of Shorter's house or Bill Hill's, no one would associate it with me.

"Okay," I said. I opened the door, and Deeks went right over me, taking no chances on getting left behind.

"You rascal." I got out and closed the car door. To his credit, Deeks was waiting for me, ready to follow wherever I might lead—and in fact he stayed right with me as we walked along the bar ditch at the side of the road.

"Maybe I don't give you enough credit," I said. "Maybe you're really a well-behaved dog."

His tail thumped the side of my leg.

Still in my stealth mode, I let us into Bill Hill's backyard on the side of the house opposite Melissa Stimmler's. When we got to the chain-link fence that separated Bill's backyard from Melissa's, I said to Deeks, "You could jump this fence—couldn't you, boy?"

He was getting enough size on him that he probably could, but maybe the dark in a strange neighborhood wasn't the place to start. I fingered the twisted spikes that protruded above the fence's top bar, looking down at him.

"Okay." I bent next to him to put a forearm under his body just behind his front legs and another just in front of his back, then straightened, raising him like I was a human forklift. I had to hunch my shoulders and stand on tiptoes to get his legs over the fence; then I bent over the fence to lower him as much as I could. When the spikes started digging into my ribs, I had to let him go. He landed softly and did a quick circle to scout out the surroundings as I put a hand to the top bar of the fence and vaulted over, scissoring my right leg over, then my left.

Deeks joined me as I climbed the steps onto Melissa's back porch. Her kitchen light was on, illuminating the curtained window panes in the back door. I tapped on the glass. There was no response. I got out my phone. I'd used her phone to email myself her photos, so I had her number.

"Hey, Melissa. It's me Robin," I typed. I pushed "Send" and waited.

"Ms. Starling?" Her frightened voice sounded from just inside the door.

"Yes. Robin," I said. "Sorry to approach you like this."

The door opened a couple of inches.

"I didn't want to get you in bad with your neighbors by coming and going through the front door." Deeks, who was, if possible, less patient than I, put his nose in the crack and pushed. Melissa jumped back from the door with a small cry, one hand going to her throat. It looked as though she wore the same housecoat she'd been wearing the last time I saw her.

"Sorry," I said. "I should have mentioned I brought company." Deeks hadn't stayed for introductions but had trotted past Melissa into her living room and disappeared. "It's my dog, Deacon. I call him Deeks, mostly, because Deacon seemed like too big a name for the little puppy I started with a few months ago."

Deeks reentered the kitchen, his tail wagging, and stopped in front of Melissa, looking up.

"If you wanted to scratch the top of his head, he'd like that," I said. "But you don't have to. Deeks!"

He didn't even glance in my direction, just stayed where he was, his eyes on Melissa as he awaited his due.

Tentatively, she reached out a pale hand, ready to snatch it back. Deeks didn't react when the tips of her fingers touched his head, but the cadence of his tail wagging did pick up a notch as she moved her fingers back and forth against his skull.

"Hello, Deeks," she whispered.

Deeks gave her housecoat a lick and came back to me.

"Okay," I told him. I looked up at Melissa. "Do you have more Sleepytime?"

"Of course." She hesitated, then picked the kettle off the stove and took it to the sink.

"Larkin was on the witness stand today," I told her. "I don't guess he's been by this evening."

Her thin back stiffened under the housecoat as she put the kettle on the stove and turned on the gas.

"The reason I ask, I used your pictures. I'm afraid there was no hiding where I got them."

She didn't look at me, just got down two mugs and the box of tea.

"He said he saw Bob Shorter the day Bill Hill died and that he was coming out of Bill Hill's house."

She separated the tea bags and put them in the mugs, then turned, finally, one hand on the counter as if to brace herself. "When?" she said. "When did he see him?"

"About four o'clock. He said Shorter had blood on him."

"Do you believe him?"

"No. Do you?"

She shook her head. Steam began rise from the spout of the kettle.

"Because you saw both Shorter and Bill Hill after that."

"Yes."

"Anyway, I gave Larkin a pretty hard time on the witness stand. My fear is he might take it out on you."

The kettle began to whistle. As Melissa took it off the stove and poured the boiling water over the tea bags in our mugs, I said, "I also came by to say thank you. Your pictures were a great help." We sat at her small Formica table, spoons in our mugs and a saucer between us. Deeks got up from his position in front of the back door and resettled at my feet.

"How worried are you about your neighbors, Jenn and Val and the rest of them?"

"What do you mean?"

"If you've still got any reserves of resolve, I could use another favor."

She looked so vulnerable, sitting there in her housecoat and looking at me with those wide eyes. I almost couldn't say it, but I did. "I'd like you to testify about seeing Bill Hill on his patio the evening of the day he died—and I've got an idea that could take you off the hook with your neighbors. If I served you with a subpoena, you'd have to go. You could show it to your neighbors, complain about me barging into your home waving papers, put the whole thing on me."

It was time to stop talking. I did, waiting for her response. Finally, she said, "You would do that? Force me to testify?"

I found I couldn't meet her gaze. "Your testimony could be so important. Shorter walking by the house while Bill was sitting in his backyard . . . those are significant facts. It was halfway through the time period the coroner has established for Bill's time of death."

I expected an argument or at least some kind of response from her, but when none was forthcoming, I spooned my tea bag onto the saucer between us and took a sip from my mug.

"You know he killed him. Mr. Shorter," Melissa said into her tea.

I looked up. "No," I said. "I know he's a bad man. I know it, you know it, everyone in the neighborhood knows it. The one thing we don't know is that he killed Bill Hill." I reached out to lay a hand over hers. "That's what trials are for, to decide questions like that. It's our job to get the facts in front of the jury to give them the best possible basis for the decision they have to make."

"Your job." She said it so softly that I leaned forward, not completely sure of what she'd said.

I sat back. "Well, yes. My job—but not just mine. It's the responsibility of all of us as citizens."

"Truth, no matter who it's for or against." She looked up finally and met my gaze. "I have something to show you." She took her phone from the pocket of her housecoat. When she'd found what she wanted, she handed it to me. "This was last July."

I was looking at a photograph of a man holding an upraised stick over a cringing dog. The man looked like Shorter.

"The dog ran up to him wagging its tail," Melissa said. "I was at the window, and I saw it all."

The dog looked like some kind of shepherd mix. "Are there more pictures?"

"Tap the screen."

It was a video. I tapped the screen, and the stick came down, catching the dog soundlessly across its back. The picture shook and a woman sobbed as the stick came down five or six more times, the man stepping after the dog as it tried to get away. Finally, the dog stopped moving. The man stood looking down at it, then looked up at the camera and pointed with the ax handle.

Melissa whispered, "He saw me. He saw me with the phone, taking pictures of him beating that dog."

I looked down at Deeks, thinking not only about him but about all the dogs I had treated when working with my father as his veterinary assistant. Quite a few of those had been shepherd mixes.

"I've been so scared."

I nodded, feeling a stab of empathy that was almost painful.

"There's no reason Mr. Shorter wouldn't have killed Bill, if he'd felt like it," Melissa said.

I sighed out a breath I didn't know I'd been holding. "No, there's not," I said. "Maybe the only question is, did he feel like it?"

"There's another question. If Mr. Shorter didn't do it, who did? Bill didn't have much in the way of friends—mostly me, and I wasn't much—but he didn't have any enemies, either."

"Except for Bob Shorter," I said.

She nodded. "There's no one else. You see that, don't you?"

I opened my mouth to talk about Shorter's right to a presumption of innocence, his right to be tried by people with open minds, but they were just platitudes. Applied to Shorter they seemed empty and even wrong. "Did he come to the door that day?" I asked. "Has he tried to hurt you?"

She shook her head. "When he walks by the house, he does that, though. Still. If he sees me in the window, he stops and points his equalizer at me, just like you saw."

"This wasn't Bill Hill's dog, was it? This was another one."

"Yes."

I stood up, and Deeks scrambled to his feet, his toenails audible on the linoleum floor. "I won't bother you anymore," I said. "If Larkin Entwistle harasses you at all, if any of them do, give me a call. I'll take care of it."

Melissa studied my face a moment. She nodded, and I left, the subpoena I'd brought with me still in the pocket of my jacket.

Chapter 16

Usually, I open my eyes in the morning and I'm awake, but the next morning my customary alertness and energy just weren't there. I shrugged into a robe and took my bottle of water into the backyard so Deeks could take care of his business without a lot of effort on my part.

I dropped into one of the patio chairs as Deeks, having paused for a quick piddle, scampered to the chain-link fence that ran along the alley, going from one corner of the backyard to the other as he checked the alley for possible activity. Not seeing anything of interest, he ran back to me, pausing on the way to snatch up a tennis ball he had long since stripped of its felt. He dropped the ball between my feet and backed up alertly. I bent for the ball and flipped it over his head. He jumped, twisting in the air, and almost caught it, then scrambled for it in the dew-soaked grass.

He brought the ball back, and I tossed it maybe a dozen more times. "You don't ask for much—do you, buddy?" I asked him. When I stepped toward the door, he ran back toward the far corner of the yard to poop. I waited for him.

"Good boy," I told him when he came back.

His tail wagged, and he grinned at me. Probably he was just panting, his tongue lolling, but it affected me like a grin. When I went in to shower, I felt ready to face the day.

I was meeting Sarah Fleckman for coffee before court, so I got off the Downtown Expressway at the west end of Carytown. About a block before I got to the Coffee Grounds, I saw a parking spot against the curb and snagged it, then grabbed my purse and walked the rest of the way.

Inside was the noise of conversation and the smell of coffee. I took my place at the end of a line that reached nearly to the door. Brian Marshall and Whitney Foster were working the counter. I didn't see Sarah, though my watch said five after eight. She was later than I was, if she was coming.

She still hadn't shown up when I got to the register.

"Robin!" Brian said as his eyes focused on me. "How are you?" Whitney, glancing over, gave me a smile and a nod.

"Pretty well. I'm in court this morning, just dropping by for a cuppa joe to get me started."

"Still drink vanilla latte?"

"I'll take two of them this morning. Someone may join me."

He charged me for the lattes, and put an apple fritter on a paper plate for me. My mouth started to water. "Fuel for the day's battle," he said, giving me a wink. "Gratis."

It wasn't easy to manage the paper plate with its glazed ambrosia and the two coffees and still scout for a table. A couple of women started strapping on their purses and satchels, one of which looked like a diaper bag, although there was no evidence of the baby who went with it. I moved over, hovering a bit to make sure no one beat me to the table, then slid onto the bench that ran along the wall as the woman with the diaper bag was sliding out.

My first victory of the morning, one that put me on my fanny while a half-dozen other people were still standing about with their mugs and their pastries. I tried to savor it while refraining from savoring the apple fritter reflecting light from its thick glaze of sugar. The temptation was inhuman. I broke off a bit of the apple fritter and popped it in my mouth. *Oh, wow.* I broke off another bit.

What with wrestling with temptation and indulging my taste buds in an orgy of sensation, I didn't see Sarah Fleckman until she pulled out the chair across from me and sat down.

"Robin Starling," she said.

"Sarah. Thanks for meeting me." I wiped my fingers with one of the rather inadequate napkins and held out my hand.

She took it with a small moue of distaste, and her handshake was limp.

"I got you coffee," I said, nodding at the cup. "It's a vanilla latte."

She eyed it a moment before picking it up, then sipped it as if suspecting I might have laced it with battery acid.

"When we talked on the phone, you seemed to know a lot about me," I said. "Try a bit of the apple fritter. It's still warm."

"Let's just get to it, shall we?"

The fritter did look like a rat had been chewing its way into it. "Okay." I took a breath. "You need to let Mike go."

She eyed me. "Did he ask you to talk to me, or are you taking this on yourself? Why didn't he call me if he had something to say?"

"Naked women make men nervous."

"He told you about that."

"He did."

She shook her head.

"I know it hurts," I said. "I know it feels unbearable. How can you put someone you've loved, someone who's been so much a part of your life, aside and go on? Believe me—I've been there. But you've got to do it. He can't be there for you anymore. You've got to accept it. He's gone."

She was fast. A balloon of hot coffee hit me in the face before I even had time to flinch. She was on her feet, her chair overturned on the floor behind her.

"You don't know me," she said into the sudden, ringing silence. "You don't know anything about me."

Actually, I couldn't tell if the coffeehouse had gone quiet, or if I'd gone deaf. The coffee dripping from my eyelashes blurred everything around me. "The next step is a restraining order," I said. "You choose."

"You're a meddling, interfering, nosy . . ."

I stood as the small table in front of me flipped toward me, and I managed to catch it with my free hand, holding my oversize mug high in the other. Sarah's mug bounced on the tile near my feet, not breaking, but splattering my feet with what was left of her coffee. Sarah was gone. I heard the door jangle as I righted the table and set down my mug.

Whitney appeared as I was wiping the coffee and vanilla syrup from my eyes with my fingers, looking about me for another of the tiny napkins. Fortunately, Sarah's vanilla latte had cooled somewhat before her psychotic episode. The coffee was hot, but not scalding, although it was going to leave brown, sticky splotches all over my clothing. I didn't see how I was going to get cleaned up before court.

Whitney touched my arm. "We've got a sink in the back. We should be able to get most of it off."

I nodded. "Thanks." I worked my way through the crowded coffee shop behind her.

In the courtroom Ian Maxwell caught my eye and gave me a quizzical glance that reminded me the cleanup had been less than complete, but I only smiled at him. They brought Shorter in, and I pushed aside the folder of photographs I'd been perusing.

"What happened to you?" he said.

I still had coffee stains that covered most of one shoulder and spotted the front of my dress, and my face was pink in places, evidently from the heat of the coffee. What little makeup I'd put on that morning was gone.

"I was interviewing a witness," I told Shorter. "It didn't go well." I didn't meet his eyes. Having seen Melissa's video showing what he had done to the shepherd mix, I couldn't look at his coarse, orangey skin and his yellowed teeth without feeling sick.

"What witness? What are you looking at there?" He nodded at the folder lying open on the table in front of me. "Photographs of the crime scene?"

"Photographs of your closet."

"What about my closet?"

I shook my head. "You know your problem, Shorter? You don't believe in anything."

"I believe in myself."

"Look where that's got you."

"What about you?"

"What about me?"

"Do you know why that Biggs fellow hates you so much? He knows you'll do whatever you need to do to win—break the rules, violate people's rights, do whatever you need to. You acknowledge no constraints whatsoever."

"He might hate me because I got him in bad with the judge. I made it look like he was suborning perjury."

"Sure. Whatever you need to do," Shorter said.

"It's not about winning."

"No?"

"I'm for truth, no matter who tells it. I'm for justice, no matter who it's for or against."

His lip curled. "What's that, your motto?"

"It seems to be. I've found myself saying it a lot lately."

The bailiff opened the door, and the jury began filing in. "I need to concentrate," I said. I pulled the folder of police photographs toward me again. As I flipped through them, I had an uneasy feeling of something out of place, but I couldn't bring it into focus. The door behind the judge's bench opened, finally, and we stood as the bailiff proclaimed, "Oyez, Oyez."

We sat, and Maxwell called his first witness of the day.

Police Detective Ray Hernandez came to the stand wearing a houndstooth sports jacket and a shirt with an open collar. In response to Maxwell's preliminary questions, he told us his degree was in criminal justice. He had been a police officer for sixteen years and had been a detective in the homicide division for eleven. He had been involved in between 100 and 150 homicide investigations.

After establishing Hernandez's bona fides as a police detective, Maxwell went over the crime scene with him, going into more detail than he had with Officer Warren. Hernandez had been present when photographs of Bill Hill's living room were taken. The photographs showed Hill's body lying facedown on the floor, only partially on an area rug. They showed the position of the body in relation to the chair he had evidently been sitting in when he was stabbed. They showed the position of the murder weapon in relation to the body. Most damningly from my client's point of view, they showed the single word scrawled in blood on the worn wood floor: *Shorter.* Each eight-by-ten photograph was identified individually as fairly and accurately representing the crime scene when Hernandez first saw it. Each was marked as a prosecution exhibit, was introduced into evidence, and was passed to the jury. It took a long time.

Maxwell next used Hernandez to introduce the murder weapon and the incriminating fingerprints found on its handle, something he'd also done in the preliminary.

"This is some kind of paring knife?" Maxwell said, holding it up.

"Yes."

"Part of a set?"

"We think so. We seized a number of similar kitchen knives when we searched the defendant's house."

"Are these the knives?"

They all had the same handles as the murder weapon. Maxwell had them marked and introduced into evidence.

"I don't notice a paring knife among these you took from the defendant's house," Maxwell said.

"We couldn't find one."

"Going back to the paring knife you found by the victim's body. You said there was blood on it?"

"There was. We assumed it was the victim's blood, but of course we turned the knife over to the office of the chief medical examiner for DNA profiling."

Eventually, the testimony moved to the search of Shorter's house, centering on the shirt and the pair of pants bunched up against the wall where Shorter's hanging clothes mostly obscured them. Maxwell moved to have the shirt and pants admitted into evidence.

"Any objection?" Judge Cooley asked me.

"I'd like to ask a few questions on voir dire." A voir dire examination was to determine the admissibility of evidence. I wasn't going to be able to get the clothes excluded, I knew, but I was getting antsy sitting beside Shorter doing nothing while the evidence poured down on us like a dump truck's load of dirt.

Judge Cooley looked at Maxwell, shrugged. "Very well."

As I replaced Maxwell at the lectern, the judge gave me a second, sharp look over the rims of his glasses.

"Are you all right?" he asked me.

"Quite all right, Your Honor."

His mouth worked, either in amusement or in an attempt to get his dentures back into place. "You look like you decided to wear your coffee this morning."

I smiled sourly. "Fortunately, the woman I was interviewing didn't have a gun."

In the jury box, Andrew Hartman let out a bray of laughter. I was beginning to find his sense of humor a lot less amusing. I turned to Hernandez. "What did you do to determine whether the clothes you found on the floor were actually the defendant's?" I asked.

"They were the same sizes as the other shirts and pants in the closet."

"You evidently spent some time talking to the neighbors. Did you ask any of them whether he or she had ever seen the defendant wearing those clothes?"

"No."

"So conceivably, these clothes could have belonged to someone else who was about the same height and weight as Bob Shorter."

"They were in the defendant's closet," Hernandez said.

"And no one else had access to the house?"

"Not as far as we know, no."

"No spare key in the toolshed?"

"Not that we found."

"Any nails in the toolshed that might have held a key before somebody took it?"

"Objection," Maxwell said, standing. "Calls for speculation."

"Sustained."

I said, "Your Honor, could I have a moment? I want to ask the witness a question about a photograph of the closet where these clothes were found."

"Your Honor," Maxwell said, "there can be no doubt as to the admissibility of these clothes."

I waited for the judge's ruling, and he cleared his throat. "By all means," he said. "Take a moment."

I shuffled through the photographs in the folder on my table until I found the one I wanted. It wasn't one the prosecution had introduced. I hadn't planned on introducing it, either, so I had only the one copy.

"Could I approach the witness to show him this photograph?" I asked the judge, holding it up. He made a circling gesture with his hand, so I took my photograph to the witness stand and handed it to Hernandez.

"Can you identify this photograph?" I asked him.

"It's a photograph of the defendant's closet."

"It's a police photograph, isn't it, made at the time you searched his house and found these clothes that you've just identified?"

"Yes."

"Does it fairly and accurately depict the closet as it was on the day you made your search?"

It did. The closet's sliding doors were pushed to the right, and two rows of hanging clothes were visible above three pairs of shoes and a pair of slippers that looked like a couple of Chihuahuas had been at them. I had the photograph marked for identification.

"There's a spot on the photograph I'm curious about. It's on the floor, maybe a foot from the back wall of the closet. Do you see it?" It was a spot that wasn't on my own photographs of the closet taken some days later.

"I see it," Hernandez said.

"Can you tell us what it is?"

He took a moment. "I think it's an old aspirin tin," he said.

"There was a pillbox listed on the search inventory and return you signed. Would that be it?"

"Probably."

"So you took the pillbox when you made the search. Can you tell us why?"

He shrugged. "It was there. It was something you wouldn't expect to find on the floor of someone's closet."

"Like the blood-spotted clothes shoved back against the wall where no one could see them?"

"Like the clothes."

"Did you look inside the pillbox? Did it contain aspirin?"

"I don't think it did. It seems like it was some other kind of pill, two or three of them."

"Capsules?"

"I seem to remember pills."

"Prescription pills of some kind?"

"Yes, though I couldn't tell you what they were."

Maxwell said, "Your Honor, these questions seem to be going rather far afield. This isn't the time for Ms. Starling's cross-examination. It's voir dire on the admissibility of the clothing."

"Your point is well taken," Judge Cooley said. "Ms. Starling?"

"I'm done, Your Honor." I had done what damage I could, which, as you may have noticed, was nil. I sat down, and the shirt and pants were admitted into evidence. Hernandez testified that, like the knife, the clothes had been delivered to the office of the chief medical examiner for DNA profiling of the blood on them.

"Now you may cross-examine," Maxwell told me.

I got up. "Detective Hernandez, you testified about fingerprints on this paring knife you found. Are you able to tell us about other fingerprints that were found inside the house of Bill Hill?"

"Yes."

"Of your own knowledge?"

"I was there when the prints were lifted and photographed, and there when the comparisons were made."

Bob Shorter had assured me in graphic terms that he had not been inside Hill's house in eight years, not since the night he had left Bill Hill afoot in a snowstorm. I believed him, not because I thought he wouldn't lie if it suited him, but because Maxwell hadn't called any crime scene technicians to testify about finding his fingerprints in the murder house. So far, there had only been Hernandez's testimony about the one set of prints found on the beechwood handle of the murder weapon. "So whose fingerprints were found inside the Hill house, other than Mr. Hill's own?"

"Just the defendant's prints on the murder weapon."

"None anywhere else in the house?"

"None anywhere else," Hernandez said. It was what I needed for my closing argument, so I left that point and went on.

"There was another fingerprint on the beechwood handle, wasn't there? One that did not belong to the defendant."

Hernandez shifted. "There was. A smudged print."

"One that you haven't been able to identify."

"No, though we think it came from one of the decedent's fingers."

"Bill Hill's? I thought he was wearing gloves."

"He was when we found him."

"And there were not enough points of similarity to establish that the print did, in fact, come from the decedent, were there?

"No."

"But you do know that the print was not made by the defendant Bob Shorter."

He did know that. I asked a few more questions about the print. I don't know that I fairly raised the possibility that the knife had been handled by person or persons unknown, but I did my best.

"Did Bill Hill have anything in his pockets when his body was found?"

"Yes. A wallet, a key ring, some change."

"No comb?"

Hernandez shook his head, a bemused half smile on his face. "I don't believe so, no. Of course, he didn't have much hair."

"Where are those items now?"

Hernandez looked at Maxwell, then back at me. "They should be in the evidence locker at police headquarters."

"Okay. Let's go back to your search of Mr. Shorter's house. I asked you about the police photograph of the defendant's closet that showed a pillbox on the floor. Was any photograph taken of the contents of that pillbox?"

"No, I don't believe there was."

"Where is the pillbox now?"

"Also in the evidence locker."

I looked up at the judge. "Your Honor, it's almost noon. Could we take our lunch recess now to give this witness the opportunity to bring those objects to court?"

"Which objects are those?" Judge Cooley asked, looking at the clock.

"The pillbox found on the floor of the defendant's closet and the contents of Bill Hill's pockets."

"Your Honor," Maxwell objected. "Counsel has no idea what she hopes to prove by these items. It's obviously a fishing expedition, and it's a waste of the court's time."

"Maybe so, but it is almost noon," Judge Cooley said. I wondered if he was thinking about the comfy sofa he had in chambers.

"I would also welcome the chance to change my clothes," I said. "I keep smelling coffee."

Again that bray of laughter from the jury box. The judge smiled.

"Very well." He banged his gavel. "Court is recessed until two o'clock. The witness will have the requested items when he resumes his testimony."

When I got back to the defense table, Shorter asked, "Are you onto something? What's significant about a comb?"

I flashed him a smile. "It is a fishing expedition," I said. "I'm hoping to land us a nice, big trout."

The momentarily hopeful expression soured on his face, but I was already looking past him. Brooke Marshall had slipped into the gallery, and she carried a paper bag with handles. With any luck, the bag contained some clean clothes for me.

Chapter 17

Ray Hernandez returned to the witness stand, and the judge reminded him that he had already been sworn. "Ms. Staring," he said, turning the floor over to me.

He'd gotten my name wrong again—misled, I can only assume, by my big blue eyes—but I didn't correct him. "Do you have the pillbox?" I asked Hernandez.

"I do." He set a plastic bag on the rail. Inside was a small yellow rectangle that said, "Bayer." It was an aspirin tin.

"Were you able to get any prints off the box?"

"No, everything was too smeared."

"Did you try?"

He smiled. "Over the lunch hour."

"So it would be all right to handle it?"

"It wouldn't destroy any evidence, if that's what you mean."

"Open it, please. Let's see what's inside."

He opened the plastic bag and took out the tin, then pinched the corners of the tin so that it popped open. "There are two pills inside," he said.

"Identical to each other?"

"Yes. Two capsule-shaped tablets with R-P-R-hypen-2-0-2 printed on one side."

"Do you know what drug that is?"

"Not a clue."

"Or what the drug is prescribed to treat?"

"No."

I had the aspirin tin marked for identification and moved to have it admitted into evidence.

"Your Honor," Maxwell said, "I don't know what counsel is getting at, but this isn't proper cross-examination. Counsel will have an opportunity to present her case after the commonwealth rests."

I said, "On direct examination, this witness testified about the contents of the defendant's closet. You can't put in pants and a shirt and refuse to consider an item lying right next to them that might have fallen from one of the pockets."

"Is that your contention?" Judge Cooley asked me. "That this item fell out of one of the pockets in the clothes that have been admitted into evidence?"

"Not necessarily. The pillbox might have been placed there on the floor deliberately. Either way, it would be significant."

"I'll grant your motion."

Since I seemed to be on a roll, I got Bill Hill's wallet and his ring of keys marked for identification and admitted into evidence while I was at it.

"No further questions," I said.

"Any redirect?"

"No, Your Honor," Maxwell said.

"Call your next witness."

I turned back to the defense table and saw that Paul and Mike had come in: They were sitting with Brooke just beyond the rail. I gave them a perfunctory smile, noticing Paul's intent expression and Mike's look of puzzlement. Shorter pushed a yellow pad in front of my chair and tapped it with a yellowed fingernail. In the middle of the page was written, "Did you land your trout or didn't you?"

I shook my head. Underneath his question I wrote, "Not a nibble," and pushed the legal pad back to him. He rolled his eyes upward as he sat back in his chair.

"Call Tara Nelson."

Tara was a technician with the forensic unit. Maxwell used her to establish that if none of Shorter's prints were found in Bill Hill's house other than those on the murder weapon, nobody else's were, either. There was no fiber or other trace evidence to suggest anyone other than Bill Hill and Bob Shorter had ever been in the house.

I'd met Tara before. She was an attractive woman in her midthirties with dark, shoulder-length hair. When it was my turn to cross-examine, I asked her, "You're telling us the defendant left no trace evidence in that house?"

"Other than the prints on the knife, none that we found."

"Doesn't that strike you as remarkable?"

"Not particularly. It does suggest the defendant didn't spend long in the house."

"Or maybe that he was never there at all," I said.

"He did carry blood from the crime scene on his clothes back to his house."

"You're assuming that it was the defendant who carried the clothes back to his house and not a third party."

"Yes."

This wasn't going well. I decided to cut my losses. "No further questions."

"I have a few questions on redirect, Your Honor," Maxwell said.

The judge inclined his head.

"Ms. Nelson. Can you tell us whether the clothes found in the defendant's house were fresh? Had they been worn after the last time they were laundered?"

She smiled. "Yes, they had. There were creases at the hips and back of the knees and two short hairs inside one of the pant legs."

"Leg hairs?"

"I think so."

"How did you connect them to the defendant?"

"I didn't. I turned them over to the office of the chief medical examiner to do a DNA profile."

I'd been right to stop my questioning. Maxwell hadn't asked about the leg hairs on direct because he had hoped that I'd bring it out—and that, coming from me, the additional connection of the bloody clothes to Bob Shorter would make more of an impact on the jury. As it was, the impact was great enough. Maxwell got Tara Nelson to identify two hairs in a plastic bag that was marked for identification and then admitted into evidence. I couldn't think of an objection that could keep them out, so I remained silent.

At the table, Shorter leaned toward me so far that when I turned toward him, our foreheads were all but touching. "I don't always wash my clothes," he whispered in an invisible cloud of stale tobacco smoke.

I frowned, blinking as my eyes began to water.

"After I wear them," he said. "Sometimes, if they're not too dirty, I drape them on the bed or even hang them back up in the closet to wear again."

I switched to mouth breathing. In a stuffy voice I said, "So you're saying that anyone who had access to your clothes would have access to clothes you'd been wearing."

"Right. So her testimony doesn't mean anything."

I wasn't so sure. How was I going to get how Shorter handled his dirty clothes into evidence without putting him on the witness stand?

"You've said that you did a thorough dusting for fingerprints inside Bill Hill's house," Maxwell was saying. "Did you also dust for prints inside the defendant's house?"

This time I did object. "That's not proper redirect, Your Honor. On cross I asked nothing about prints inside the defendant's house." I hadn't asked, because I knew from the police reports what was coming: No prints had been found inside Shorter's house other than his own. Their absence didn't disprove my theory of a frame-up, but it didn't help, either.

The judge looked over his glasses at Maxwell. "Counselor?"

Maxwell tongue slid across his lower lip. He was caught. "She did ask about the witness's examination of the defendant's clothes, which were inside the house."

I said, "I did not ask about her examination of the defendant's clothes. You yourself asked those questions."

"Could we have the court reporter read back Ms. Starling's last question?" Maxwell said.

The judge nodded. "Mr. Yielding?"

Mr. Yielding found the question and read, "You're assuming that it was the defendant who carried the clothes back to his house and not a third party. Answer: Yes."

Maxwell was silent, thinking. I said, "That is not a question about her examination of clothes. Rather, it's a question about an assumption of the witness that goes to bias."

Judge Cooley nodded. "I'll sustain the objection."

After a moment, Maxwell nodded. "No further questions."

His next witness was one I'd been expecting almost from day one: Dr. Harold Pavlicek, a pathologist with the office of the chief medical examiner. He told us that death had occurred in the afternoon or evening of March 9. "Death was brought about by a stab wound to the chest," he said.

"Did the stab wound pierce the heart?"

"No, the blade missed the heart, though it did damage the left coronary artery. There was a great deal of bleeding, both internal and external."

"Would death have been instantaneous in such a case?" Maxwell asked.

"No, it would not. And in this particular case, the extensive bleeding shows us that death could not have been instantaneous, because, once the heart stops, bleeding slows considerably. Here the decedent lived for probably twenty or thirty minutes after the wound was inflicted."

"But the stab wound was the cause of death?"

"Oh, yes."

"Did you prepare a DNA profile of the decedent's blood?"

He had.

"And a DNA profile of the blood found on a shirt and a pair of pants that were given to you by the police?"

"Yes."

"A DNA profile of two leg hairs that came from that pair of pants?"

"Two leg hairs delivered to me by one Tara Nelson."

"I show you Prosecution Exhibit 19 and ask if you can identify it."

"That's the shirt given to me by police for purposes of DNA comparison."

"The shirt with blood on it."

"Yes."

"Can you identify Prosecution Exhibit 20?" Maxwell exhibited the pair of bloodstained khakis.

Dr. Pavlicek could.

"Prosecution Exhibit 21?" It was the paring knife.

"Yes, it was given to me for purposes of doing a DNA comparison between the reference sample and the blood on it."

"And did you complete a DNA comparison with each of these items?"

"Yes, I did. The reference sample and the unknown samples from the shirt and pants were all a match. The blood on the clothes was William Hill's."

Maxwell went through the same questions with respect to the murder weapon. Unsurprisingly, the blood on the knife was also William Hill's.

"This baggie containing two small hairs has been entered into evidence as Prosecution Exhibit 28. What can you tell me about it?"

"It, too, was given to me to make a DNA comparison between them and a reference sample."

"Was this reference sample also blood drawn from William Hill's body?"

"It was not. This time the reference sample was blood drawn from the body of the defendant in this case, Robert Shorter."

"And what was the result of the comparison?"

"The two small hairs came from the body of Robert Shorter."

Maxwell finished with his direct examination of Dr. Pavlicek at two minutes before five. With a glance at the clock, Judge Cooley tapped his gavel and stood. "Courts adjourned until nine o'clock tomorrow."

So I left the courthouse with Paul and Mike and Brooke. Nobody said anything until we had cleared the doors and were out in a strong April breeze that whipped at my clothing. Then Mike said, "So. Brooke tells me you talked to Sarah."

"I did. That's how I came to be wearing a vanilla latte perfume."

"Sorry about that."

"Me, too. On the other hand, maybe that was the final cathartic moment when she found she was able to give you up."

"You think so?"

"We can hope. I think I've done all I can do, unless you want to hire me to get a restraining order."

"I guess I could do that myself."

"But you won't," Brooke said.

"I will if it's necessary," Mike said.

"If she comes back, I'll hire you, Robin," Brooke said.

Mike took a breath as if he might say something, but he let it out again without speaking.

"Where shall we eat?" Paul said. "Mike's buying."

"I am?"

"Robin's wearing that vanilla latte perfume."

"Good point," Mike said.

"I'd really like to take a shower before dinner," I said.

"Great," Paul said. "We can pick a place out near you. How about Italian?"

We were at my car, and I beeped it open. "Mario's?" I said as I got in. "Paul likes the house Chianti. Seven o'clock?"

"Uh, Robin," Brooke said as I reached for my seat belt.

I glanced down and saw what she meant. I gave the hem of my dress a tug in the direction of my knees, but my dress had gotten bunched beneath me. I pushed my feet against the floorboard to get my butt off the seat and tried again. "Oh, give it up, all of you," I said. "Don't pretend you've never seen a woman's panties before."

With that inauspicious exit line, I pulled my door shut and headed for home.

It was ten o'clock before Deeks and I headed out for our run. I was jogging at a medium pace, and Deeks, off leash, was checking out the shrubbery on my side of the road and roughly keeping pace. When I turned a corner, a trail of sparks arched toward me, and a report like a gunshot sounded just in front of my right knee. I jumped sideways, twisting, turning in a full circle to keep from falling. *Not a gunshot,* I thought. A firecracker or something like it. I crouched in the road, trying to discern shapes in the darkness around me.

"Stahling," called a voice somewhere off to my right. "Stahhhling." The house on that side of me was a shadow half-hidden in the larger shadow of an overgrown magnolia. I started as something cold touched my neck above the collar of my sweatshirt, but it was Deeks, who had come back to me out of the darkness.

"Bitch," came a hoarse whisper. I turned, but there was nothing behind me. The word was repeated, this time somewhere ahead of me and to my left. The situation was every bit as creepy as it sounds. Maybe it was dangerous. I didn't know.

"Stay close, buddy," I murmured, and Deacon replied with a soft whine.

The limbs of the magnolia tree rattled.

"Easy," I said.

Something fizzed behind me as I sensed movement on my left.

"Go," I said. I sprinted forward as the exploding firework sounded just behind my head. Within a few steps, I was running full-out, Deeks at my heel. A shadow loomed out of the darkness on my left, then we were by it, and the road was clear ahead.

At the next corner, I stuttered a step in order to turn right without tripping over my dog. "Deeks!"

He made the turn with me.

I turned into the next alley and bent over by a trash container, breathing hard, my hands braced on my knees. Deeks licked my face. I curled my fingers into his collar. The alley, except for us, was empty.

I waited, my eyes on the spot where the alley intersected the street, but no one appeared. *The wicked flee where none pursueth*, I thought. It wasn't Shakespeare. Holy writ, maybe. Even if no one was behind me now, though, I had been pursued. My ears still rang with the sound of that second firecracker.

When I stood up, I winced at the stiffness in my legs. Deeks, evidently feeling that things had returned to normal, began checking out the trash containers and various fence posts as we continued down the alley. I stopped walking, and he came back to me, looked up into my face.

"What do you think, buddy? Are we safe?"

His tail wagged.

"What do you know?"

He extended his neck to reach his head forward and lick my knee. I laughed.

"Good dog," I told him. "Let's go home."

When I got close, I changed my mind. I didn't want to go home. People knew where I lived—if not everyone, at least everyone who knew how to use a phone book. Changing direction, I found the alley that ran behind Dr. McDermott's house and let Deeks and me through the gate into his backyard.

"Give a bark and let him know we're out here," I told Deeks.

He didn't react.

"Speak!"

I sensed him looking at me, but it might have been my imagination. It was really too dark to tell. "Speak," I said again.

He woofed.

"He's not going to hear that. Speak!"

Deeks barked at me.

"Good boy."

As we stepped up onto the back stoop, an exterior light came on, looking elegant and somehow homey in its fixture of copper and beveled glass. The door opened. It was Dr. McDermott, the hair at the back of his head standing up like the graying plumage of some exotic bird—one with chin wattles. I giggled.

"Robin? What's wrong?" He pushed open the storm door, Deeks rushing past him through the opening door. Dr. McDermott peered past me and to each side, then stepped back, motioning me in. Deeks was already coming back from the next room.

"Everything all right in there, buddy?" I asked him.

Dr. McDermott turned from locking the door. "Is one of you going to tell me what this is all about?"

I looked at Deeks but knew it was going to have to be me. "Unwelcome company on our run," I said. "Somebody threw a couple of firecrackers at us."

"Firecrackers! That could be dangerous."

"Where did you get those pants? They're hilarious." He was wearing a pair of plaid pants made from baggy flannel with elastic at the ankles.

"What's wrong with them? They're my lounging britches."

"A name almost as funny as they are. How come I've never seen them?"

"I don't know. Maybe I'll model my entire wardrobe for you someday. First, though, we need to decide what to do. Call the police? Or I can get my pistol, and we'll go check out your house."

"Not the police," I said, shaking my head. "I really think all this will go away once the trial's over."

"Would you and Deacon like to stay here tonight?"

"I don't know. Is your guest room available?"

He smiled at me. "It is always available for you," he said.

Chapter 18

I woke to the smell of coffee and frying bacon. When I'd eaten more than was good for me, Dr. McDermott got his pistol and crossed the street with Deeks and me and stood guard in the living room while I showered and got dressed for court. When I came out, he was pacing, his head swiveling and eyes alert, as if an army of commandos might come crashing through the windows at any moment.

"I'll see you out through the garage. Then I'll lock up after myself," he said.

I shook my head at him, smiling. "You are a sweetie."

He wasn't the only sweetie. The first person I saw when I got off the courthouse elevator was Melissa Stimmler, sitting on one of the benches on the second floor, her small hands clenched in her lap.

I sat beside her. "You are a brave woman," I said.

"I'm not. I'm a terrified woman who's ashamed of herself."

"That counts as bravery in my book."

Her smile seemed pale. "I'm not here for him, not even for you, really. I'm here for . . . for truth no matter who tells it and justice no matter who it's for or against."

I really needed to figure out where that quote came from.

"I would like that subpoena, though, to show Val and Jenn when they get after me."

I fished it out of my briefcase and filled it in for her. "Thank you," I said. "I'll stick with my original observation. You're a brave woman."

More people were getting off the elevator now, some going into Judge Cooley's courtroom, some going into the clerk's office, some going into the other courtroom. Others collected in small groups to talk in awe-muted voices. I put my arm around Melissa to give her a hug.

"There's a special room for witnesses to stay in until they're called. It may be empty. At any rate, your neighbors have testified and gone. There shouldn't be anyone there to give you problems."

"I brought some reading." She opened her purse and pulled out a copy of *Reader's Digest.*

"I didn't know they still published that."

"They still do." She held it up, pointing at the date, which was the current month. "Actually, it's my mother's subscription. I never canceled it." She lowered her voice as if about to impart a shameful secret. "What I like best are the jokes. I cut out my favorites and keep them." She wet her lips, hesitating. "When all this is over, maybe you and Deeks could come over for tea again, and we could read some of them."

"We'd like that, very much." I met her gaze, and she smiled at me.

"It's about to start. Let me show you to the witness room," I said.

Court reconvened, and Dr. Harold Pavlicek returned to the stand. Judge Cooley said, "Mr. Maxie, I believe you had just finished with your direct examination?"

"Maxie is a woman's name, your honor," Maxwell said, looking pained. The laugh from the jury box came from a woman this time, although Andrew Hartman smirked.

"So you have no further questions?" Judge Cooley said.

Maxwell sighed. "No further questions."

Probably I'm slow on the uptake, but it occurred to me suddenly that Judge Cooley was doing the name thing on purpose. This was his way of amusing himself at the expense of the lawyers who appeared before him.

"Ms. Startling, you may cross-examine."

I grinned at him.

"Ms. Startling, you wish to address the court?"

I shook my head. "No, Your Honor." I went to the lectern, and Dr. Pavlicek blinked at me expectantly through his round lenses. He had a half smile on his face, and it occurred to me that he was enjoying himself, too. A weight in my chest lifted that I hadn't known I was carrying. This was life, and it was a good life, so many of us working diligently to do the right thing.

"Dr. Pavlicek, why is your estimation of the time of death so imprecise? Your testimony is that death occurred sometime between noon and midnight of the ninth. Really?"

"Unfortunately, yes. When a body is discovered too long after death, body temperature is of no help to us. In this case, the body had already cooled to the temperature of the house, though the house was quite cool when I got there, right at sixty-two degrees. If the house had been at that temperature since death, and there's no reason to think it hadn't been, that means death occurred at least twenty-two hours prior to the time I took the temperature of the body, which was just before four o'clock on the afternoon of the eleventh."

"Because after twenty-two hours, the body temperature would have become constant," I said.

"That's right."

"What about rigor mortis?"

"Rigor mortis sets in two to six hours after death and lasts for maybe thirty hours after that. None of this is exact, you understand, but in this case, rigor mortis had come and gone."

"So the absence of rigor mortis tells us that Mr. Hill had been dead more than thirty-six hours. Is that right?"

Pavlicek was nodding. "Based on the body temperature and the absence of rigor mortis, I would say that Mr. Hill died before four a.m., the morning of the tenth."

"You said before midnight on the ninth."

"Yes. Other factors made me think it had been a somewhat longer than the minimum time indicated by body temperature and the departure of rigor mortis."

"The same factors that made you think he had died in the twelve hours before midnight? How do you know he hadn't been dead a week?"

"The processes of autolysis and putrefaction had begun but were not well advanced."

"Autolysis is . . ."

"A process of self-digestion begun by the living enzymes contained within the body's cells."

"And putrefaction?"

"Putrefaction results from bacteria that escape from the body's intestinal tract after death. After about thirty-six hours the skin of the trunk and head begins to develop a greenish tinge."

"And the deceased's skin had developed this tinge?"

"It had."

I hated to ask. "What's the next step in autolysis and putrefaction?"

"Bloating."

Of course it was.

"The bacteria produce gas that accumulates most visibly in the face, making the eyes and tongue protrude as the gas inside pushes them forward."

It was enough to make a girl squeamish, and I didn't see that it was getting me anywhere. I had no reason to think that Pavlicek's estimate of the time of death was off. Melissa Stimmler's testimony was going to cut his time window in half anyway, and Bob Shorter had no alibi for any relevant time period.

"Had the body been moved after death?" I asked.

"Not in my opinion, certainly not after livor mortis had begun."

I had him tell the jury what livor mortis was: the settling of the blood after the heart stopped beating, a process that darkened the body tissues closest to the floor.

"Did your examination reveal evidence of a struggle? Skin under the fingernails, defensive wounds to the palms or forearms?"

"No, nothing like that."

"I noticed from the autopsy report that there was a cut on the front of the right thigh."

"Yes, but that wasn't a defensive wound. It was a cut that had evidently occurred sometime earlier. There was a piece of tape across it, nipped in over the wound to create a makeshift butterfly bandage."

"The leg was taped so as to hold the wound closed?"

"That's right."

"Is the presence of the tape the only reason you say the cut was made sometime before the murder?"

"Well, there was no cut or a tear in the pants leg."

"What does that tell us? That the cut was made while Mr. Hill wasn't wearing any pants?"

"At least not those pants."

"Do you know anything about another pair of pants with a cut or tear in the pant leg?"

"No, though I don't think there's any reason to look for one. The blood loss was insignificant, and the wound bore no relation to the cause of death."

"When you say the blood loss was insignificant—how do you know there was any blood loss at all?"

"A small amount of blood had seeped into the fabric of the pants."

"On the inside?"

"Yes, though there was enough blood to show through the outside of the pants, too."

"The pants the decedent was wearing at the time of his death, the ones with no cut or tear in the pant leg?"

"Yes."

"So this was a recent cut, and fairly deep. Would you say this cut was made on the day of the decedent's death?"

"Yes, I would."

"What could have caused it?"

He tilted his head and raised his shoulders. "A household accident of some kind? Your guess is as good as mine."

"Could it have been done with a blade like the paring knife that's been identified as the murder weapon?"

"Certainly."

I retrieved the aspirin tin from the court reporter and took it to Dr. Pavlicek. "Could you open that aspirin tin and take a look at what's inside?"

He opened the box. "Two pills," he said.

"Do you recognize them? Can you tell us what kind of drug this is?"

"No."

I went back to the lectern to look at my notes, but there wasn't a lot more I could do with Dr. Pavlicek. "No further questions," I said, and returned to my seat.

"Mr. Maxine?" the judge said. I didn't know how he managed to keep a straight face.

Ian Maxwell was flipping pages on his yellow pad. He looked up and said, "The prosecution rests, Your Honor."

The judge looked at the clock, which read 10:55 a.m. "I assume you'll want to recess over the lunch hour before beginning your case," he said to me.

"Actually, Your Honor, I have one witness I'd like to call before lunch. Melissa Stimmler is in the witness room. I believe we can finish with her before noon."

Judge Cooley looked at the clock again. He sighed. "Very well." The bailiff slipped through the side door to get Melissa. I went to the rail. Paul and Brooke and Mike were seated together on the first row of seats, and for once our suite mate, Rodney Burns, was sitting with them. I leaned over the rail to talk to Rodney. He wasn't my closest friend of the bunch, but he was a private detective.

"How long would it take you to get copies of Bill Hill's medical records?" I asked him.

"I don't know. Who's his doctor?"

"No idea. Wait." I turned to check the folders on the table, then, not seeing what I wanted, dug another one out of my briefcase. I flipped through photographs until I came to the ones I had taken of Hill's medicine cabinet. I handed one of them to Rodney. "Here's a close-up of his prescription bottles. Does that say Dr. Gore?"

"It looks like it." He sounded uncertain.

"What a name for a doctor," I said. "Actually, here." I dug out a subpoena issued in blank and scribbled the name "Dr. Gore," a time, and "medical records of William Hill" in the appropriate blanks.

239

"We can't force him to leave his practice on such short notice, but bring him back with you if you can. I'd like him to testify."

"Testify to what?"

"I'm still working on it. Oh, and one more thing. I need the doorknob off Shorter's back door."

"I'm supposed to have all this by when?"

"Two o'clock would be good." The bailiff was back. I gave Melissa a smile and a nod as he led her to the front of the courtroom to be sworn.

"Do you at least have a key to Shorter's house?" Rodney asked.

"Oh yeah. Give me a minute." I got it from my purse.

"How do I secure the house after I've removed the doorknob?" Rodney asked.

I looked at him in exasperation.

"Okay, okay," he said, raising a hand. "I'll work it out."

"Thank you."

Paul said, "Did you know Rodney was going to be here? What would you have done if he hadn't been?"

I turned my smile on him.

"Oh. Right," he said.

Melissa stepped up into the witness box, and I went to the lectern.

"Hi, Melissa."

She regarded me with wide, anxious eyes.

"We need to start off with your full name for the record."

"Melissa Rae Stimmler." Her voice was so low that the judge leaned forward to hear her.

"Where do you live in relation to the decedent, Bill Hill? Say it as loudly as you can. There are a lot of people who need to hear you."

"Next door." Her voice was still too soft, but she cleared her throat and tried again. "Right next door to him."

"You live on the corner. He lived next to you?"

She nodded. "That's right. We've lived right next to each other since, I don't know, maybe fifteen years?" She looked up at the judge and gave him a smile that seemed apologetic.

"Did you see him very often?"

"Sometimes. Sometimes he came over for tea, not too often. He had trouble walking."

"Did you visit him?"

"It's been a few years. Our dogs used to play together in his backyard."

I sensed a stirring in the jury box. We already knew what had happened to Bill's dog. "How about more recently?" I asked.

"More recently, I'd see him when he sat out in his backyard. I'd tap on my kitchen window and wave. That wasn't too often."

"When was the last time?"

"The day . . . the day they say he died."

"The day someone killed him."

She nodded solemnly. "The day someone killed him."

"When was this? What time of day?"

"The sun had just gone down. He had a lawn chair on his patio, an old aluminum one with yellow straps that had turned brown at the ends. He was sitting there when I saw him, not doing much of anything, just sitting and thinking, it looked like. I tapped on the window, like always, and he looked up at me. I waved, and he . . . I just remembered. He kissed the ends of his fingers and held them out to me. That's strange, isn't it? It was like he was saying good-bye."

"Had he never done that before?"

"Not that I remember."

"How do you fix this date in your mind, the date this happened?"

"It was Friday. Two days later he was found dead."

"Did you see Bob Shorter that day, as well?"

Her gaze drifted to Shorter where he sat at the defense table, and she jerked it away. "Yes. I saw him. He was going by the house on one of his walks."

"So he was on the street that runs in front of your house?"

"Yes, mine and Bill's. He turns the corner and goes by my house, then Bill's, and he continues on down the street."

"And that Friday, his walk was along that same route."

She nodded.

"Yes?"

"Yes," she said.

"When was this exactly?"

"Right before I went into the kitchen and saw Bill."

"So it was dusk, just getting dark?"

"Yes. Six o'clock or so."

"Bob Shorter didn't turn toward Bill's house, just continued down the street as usual?"

"No. I don't think he even glanced at it, just walked along swinging his stick."

If Larkin's testimony about seeing a bloodied Shorter leaving Bill Hill's house at four o'clock still had any lingering credibility, her testimony should put an end to it, I thought. To drive home the point, I said, "We've heard some testimony that a couple of hours earlier Bob Shorter came out of Bill's house with blood on him. Did you see Bob Shorter coming out of Bill Hill's house earlier that day?"

"No, I didn't. I haven't seen Mr. Shorter at Bill's house in years."

"And you didn't see any blood on him that evening when you saw him?"

"No. Of course, it was getting dark."

Fair enough. "Did Bill Hill have blood on him that you saw?"

"No, but like I said, it was getting dark."

"But he didn't seem injured to you."

"Objection," Maxwell said. "Leading."

"Did he seem injured or in pain?" I asked, rephrasing the question.

"Not that I noticed."

"Thank you, Melissa. That's all I have."

Judge Cooley, his eyes on the clock, picked up his gavel and said, "It's right at the noon hour."

"It'll be just a few questions on cross-examination, Your Honor," Maxwell said, standing.

The judge rolled his eyes toward him. "Very well."

Maxwell went to the lectern. "You live next door to Bill Hill, is that right?" Although they weren't permitted on direct examination, on cross, leading questions were the standard.

"That's right." Her voice had gone soft again, as if she were retreating back into herself.

"I assume the police came by to ask you about what you saw or didn't see that day?"

"They came by."

"You didn't tell them about seeing Bill Hill in his backyard, did you?"

"I don't think I did." Her voice was even softer.

"In fact, you specifically told them you didn't see Bill Hill that day, didn't you?"

For a moment I thought she wouldn't be able to answer. Then she cleared her throat and said, in a louder voice, "No, they didn't ask me." She glanced at the judge with an anxious expression. "The police seemed mostly interested in whether I'd seen anyone going into or out of Bill's house that day, whether I'd heard anything."

"Did you make it clear to those police officers that you'd seen Bill Hill on the actual day of the murder?"

She shook her head.

"The truth is, you weren't sure what day it was you'd seen him—isn't that right?"

"I knew when it was." She was looking down into her lap now.

"But you didn't make that clear to the officers," Maxwell said.

This had gone on long enough. I stood. "Objection, Your Honor. The question has been asked and answered."

Judge Cooley peered over his glasses at Maxwell. "Is that the only question you have for this witness, Mr. Maxworth?"

Maxwell looked as frustrated as I'd ever seen him. "Just a few more, Your Honor."

"Let's get on with them then."

"Yes, Your Honor." He took a breath. "How did Ms. Starling, Mr. Shorter's attorney, find out about this sighting of yours?"

"She asked me," Melissa said.

"And you told her."

"Yes."

"But you didn't tell the police officers when they asked you?"

"Asked and answered," I objected.

"Sustained."

"How long did you speak to the police officers?" Maxwell asked the witness.

"I don't know. They might have been at the door ten or fifteen minutes."

"You didn't let them in."

She shook her head. "No, they didn't insist on it."

"But you let Ms. Starling in."

Melissa's upper lip and her eyebrows rose in an expression of wonder. "Ms. Starling can be pretty persuasive," she said.

I didn't know whether Maxwell was succeeding in his efforts to cast doubt on Melissa's testimony or whether he was just making my investigative work look more thorough than that of the police. It did seem to me that Hernandez and Jordan had missed something here. They'd settled on their theory of the case too quickly.

"Did Bill Hill spend many evenings in his backyard staring at your window?" Maxwell asked.

"He wasn't staring at my window. I had to tap on it to get his attention."

"What was he looking at?"

"I think he was looking at Mr. Shorter's house. You can see it from there, just past the end of the alley that runs behind the houses. We just have chain-link fences, Bill and I. No privacy fences or anything like that to block the view."

"Did he often sit and look at Mr. Shorter's house?"

She nodded. "Yes. All the time."

Maxwell looked at the clock. "I have no further questions."

The judge had already picked up his gavel.

"No questions on redirect," I said as the gavel fell.

"Court is adjourned until two o'clock."

The four of us—Mike, Brooke, Paul, and me—had lunch near the hospital. While we waited for our food, I texted Rodney, *How's it going?*

The response took ten minutes and, when it came, was uninformative: *It's going.*

I started to text back to ask if he could possibly be more specific, but I let it go. Rodney was a good man, and he'd do what he could. Our waitress was handing out drinks. Brooke and I had water; Paul and Mike each had a beer. As I sipped my water, I said to Paul, "Beer with waffles? Really?"

"Chicken waffles. It's Friday, and anyway, I'm taking a day's vacation."

"And beer and pizza is a classic," Mike said, taking a sip from his mug.

I looked at Brooke, and she shrugged. She was sharing Mike's pizza, but, at least for herself, obviously considered water an adequate beverage to go with it.

"Gonna wait until you're married to put him on beer rations?" I asked her.

"Now that's not helpful," Mike said.

"I'm not his mother," Brooke said.

"That's my girl." He tapped her water glass with his mug, then leaned toward her to kiss her cheek.

"Public displays of affection?" I said.

"Boy, you're critical today," Mike said. "Why are you trying to stir up trouble?"

Paul sipped his beer and wisely stayed out of it.

"Sorry," I said to Mike. "I'm feeling pressure."

"It sounds like you've got a plan. What is it?"

"To flounder around in all directions in hopes of catching hold of something that floats."

Paul said, "That sounds like you're drowning."

Brooke said, "It doesn't sound encouraging— that's for sure."

"Relax, it's her modus operandi," Mike said, but I couldn't tell if he intended the remark as encouraging or critical.

"Well thank you all for the vote of confidence."

"Don't get me wrong," Mike said. "You're the best on your feet of any lawyer I've ever seen. You do tend to work without a net, though."

"You're mixing your metaphors," I said. "Am I a boxer or an acrobat?"

"Both. I mixed my metaphors deliberately." He sipped his beer and looked smug.

When our food had come and we'd ingested a good bit of it, Brooke said, "Why do you want Shorter's doorknob? And Bill Hill's medical records? I don't see the connection."

"I should think it's obvious," I said. "You tell me."

They all looked at me, and I smiled. "Just kidding. I don't know that there is a connection."

"So what are you thinking?" Mike asked.

"At this point, I'd rather not say. I'm just pulling on every thread I can think of."

Mike and Brooke and Paul chewed thoughtfully.

"Threads you're going to use to weave a rug?" Paul asked.

Mike said, "You're pulling threads to unravel something?"

So the metaphor of pulling threads wasn't particularly enlightening. I turned to Brooke. "I'm planning to call you as my next witness. You up for it?"

She stopped chewing, then swallowed. "No. What for?"

"Nothing serious. I want to introduce the photographs you took at Bill Hill's house."

"I don't want to testify."

"I know."

She took a breath. "I'll do it," she said. "If you need me."

"Thank you. With that settled, I can relax and finish my fish tacos." I took a bite.

"I hope *you're* hungry," Brooke said to Mike, pushing the dish with the last piece of their pizza toward him.

"Sorry," I said. "I didn't mean to spoil your appetite."

"So is she on your witness list?" Mike asked, picking up his fourth piece of pizza. "Or is that going to be a problem?"

"She's on my witness list."

"You didn't tell me I was on your witness list," Brooke said.

"I didn't want to worry you."

"You've got an idea," Paul said.

"Oh, I'm full of them," I said. "Or maybe just full of it. We'll see."

"Ms. Starving," the judge said, "call your next witness." I didn't know how many possible mispronunciations of my name there were, but surely by now Judge Cooley had worked through just about all of them.

"Starling," I said.

"Yes, of course. Starling."

I looked back over the gallery, but Rodney Burns still had not returned.

"Call Brooke Marshall," I said.

She stood and pushed through the bar, looking as cool as lemonade. When she'd been sworn and taken her seat, though, she looked at me reproachfully.

"Could you tell us your name, please?" I asked.

She told us.

"Your occupation?"

When we had the preliminaries out of the way, I distributed copies of photographs I had brought with me to the lectern. I showed Brooke one of them. "Could you tell us what this photograph is?"

"It's a photograph of the inside of Bill Hill's medicine cabinet."

"Who took it?"

"You did."

"Does the photograph fairly and accurately represent the inside of the medicine cabinet as it existed on the afternoon of March 26, the day we walked through Mr. Hill's house with two police officers?"

"It does." After a pause, she added, "None of us took anything out of the medicine cabinet or added anything to it, if that's what you're asking."

"It wasn't, but thank you. That's very helpful." After the photograph had been marked for identification, I presented her with another one. "Can you tell us what this photograph is?"

"A close-up of Mr. Hill's prescription medications in that same medicine cabinet."

That photograph too fairly and accurately represented what we had seen on March 26. I got her to authenticate one more photograph, then moved to admit them into evidence.

Maxwell objected. "I don't see the relevance, Your Honor."

"Ms. Staving?" Okay, the judge had found one more.

"I'll connect it up, Your Honor."

"Then I'll wait to rule on your motion until you do."

"No further questions," I said.

Maxwell stood. Brooke's testimony was so limited in scope that there wasn't much he could do with it on cross-examination. "No questions, Your Honor."

As I got back to the defense table, Rodney Burns and another man came through the door, Rodney with a box under his arm. I met his gaze and gave him a nod. He jerked his head at the bald, red-faced man who had come in with him, and I smiled.

I turned back to the judge. "Call Dr. Richard Gore."

Unlike Melissa Stimmler, Brooke Marshall, and Rodney Burns, all of whom I had listed in an abundance of caution, Dr. Gore was not on my witness list. Maxwell objected, and we had a bench conference.

"I didn't expect to call Dr. Gore until he walked into the courtroom just now," I said. "At best, I was hoping to introduce some of his records. Bill Hill was his patient."

"Your Honor, not only is this an unfair surprise to the prosecution, but I fail to see any relevance of this witness to the question of whether or not the defendant killed Bill Hill."

"As I promised, I'm trying to connect up those photographs that were just marked for identification. I would have had Dr. Gore on the witness list, but it was only today that I realized how important his testimony was going to be to the defendant's case."

"Important in what way?" Judge Cooley asked me.

I would have liked to be able to tell him, but actually I was still working on that. "I'm sorry it's a surprise to Mr. Maxwell, but I don't think he's going to find himself disadvantaged. If he's right about the relevance of the testimony, the worst we're looking at is a waste of time. It will be a bigger waste of time, though, if I have to try to get at the same facts through the people whose names are on my witness list."

Judge Cooley raised his chin to look at me through the lenses of his wire-rimmed glasses.

"If I can call Dr. Gore, I expect to rest my case by the end of the day," I said. "Otherwise, it will be tomorrow afternoon at the earliest."

That clinched it. The judge overruled the prosecution's objection, and Dr. Gore came to the witness stand.

"Hi," I said to him. "I'm Robin Starling. Could you tell us your name?"

"Richard Gore."

He didn't put the "Dr." in front of his name, which gave me an instant liking for him. Though I've called him bald, he wasn't completely. He had a fringe of reddish-blond hair, and his pudgy face had a boyish look that I found appealing. "Your profession?" I asked him.

"I'm a neurologist."

"We appreciate your taking time out of your busy practice to come talk to us today."

He smiled perfunctorily. "Actually, I didn't have any patients scheduled after four, and my last one called to cancel while I was talking to your detective. I wouldn't have missed it, really. This will give me something to tell my boys at the dinner table."

"We'll try not to make it too noteworthy. Did you know William Hill during his lifetime, Dr. Gore?"

"He was my patient. I was treating him for amyotrophic lateral sclerosis, more commonly known as ALS or Lou Gehrig's disease."

"Could you tell us about the progression of the disease in Mr. Hill's case?"

Dr. Gore took a breath and exhaled it. "Bill was diagnosed about a year and a half ago. An electromyogram showed nerve damage. Other tests ruled out muscular dystrophy, multiple sclerosis, spinal cord tumors, and a few other possibilities. Over the next eighteen months, he continued to get progressively weaker. His arms and legs stiffened, and he lost muscle mass. His biggest problems were increased difficulty in speaking and swallowing. We'd begun to talk about what he would do when independent living was no longer possible."

"How long did he have to live?"

"It's hard to say. People generally live from two to five years after diagnosis, but Mr. Hill was likely to be at the lower end of that range."

"So at the time of his death he might not have had more than six months to live," I said.

"He might not have."

"What do ALS patients ultimately die of?"

"Respiratory failure, usually hastened by aspiration pneumonia."

Maxwell stood. "I don't see the relevance of this line of questioning. Is counsel suggesting that Mr.

Hill's murder was a mercy killing? That's not a valid defense, and she knows it."

"Your Honor," I said. "Dr. Gore's testimony is part of the res gestae. If I'm allowed to proceed, I can connect it up."

"I'll overrule the objection."

"Thank you." I showed Dr. Gore the close-ups of the prescription drugs in Bill Hill's medicine cabinet. "Are these medications that you were prescribing for Mr. Hill?" I asked him.

"Yes, most of them."

"Could you walk us through them, tell us what each was for?"

"Sure." He held the photograph a little farther away and tilted his head so that he was looking through the bottom part of his glasses. "Baclofen is a muscle relaxer, which I prescribed to help with pain and muscle stiffness. Phenytoin is an anticonvulsant that also helped with cramps. Elavil is a tricyclic antidepressant to control excess saliva production and help with involuntary drooling. Rilutek decreases serum glutamate, which is an amino acid that often increases in ALS patients to the point that it damages nerve cells. This bottle labeled BCAA is actually a nutritional supplement to help with muscle decline and weight loss. Cymbalta was to help with Mr. Hill's depression . . ." It turned out that at the time of his death, Bill Hill had been taking pretty much everything in his medicine cabinet on a daily basis.

"There was some kind of breathing machine by Mr. Hill's bed," I said. "Would that have been related to his ALS?"

Dr. Gore nodded. "A BiPAP machine to help him breathe at night."

I retrieved the aspirin tin from the court clerk. "Could you tell us what this is?"

"Some kind of pillbox," he said. "It says aspirin."

"Could you open it and tell us if it actually contains aspirin?"

He opened it. "It does not. There are two pills here, both of them Rilutek."

"That would be one of the drugs you prescribed for Mr. Hill?"

"It would."

"Thank you, Dr. Gore. That will be all."

The aspirin tin had gotten Maxwell's attention. He went to the lectern. "I remain puzzled by the purpose of your testimony," he said.

Dr. Gore smiled at him, blinking through his glasses. "As do I."

Maxwell looked at him thoughtfully another moment, then picked back up his legal pad. "Never mind," he said. "I have no questions of this witness."

I stood and watched as Dr. Gore pushed through the bar and took a seat in the gallery, possibly hoping for more to tell his boys at the dinner table. "Call Rodney Burns," I said.

He came forward with the cardboard box, setting it on the defense table on his way to the witness stand. As he was being sworn, I looked in the box and saw a keyed doorknob and a dead bolt.

"Hello," I said, giving him my patented put-the-witness-at-ease smile. "Could you give us your full name, please?"

He didn't smile back. Rodney Burns was a phlegmatic cuss. "Rodney Burns," he said.

"Your address and occupation?"

"Ten-eleven East Main Street." It was his business address, the same as mine. "I'm a private investigator licensed by the Virginia Department of Criminal Justice Services."

"Have you been employed as a private investigator today, Mr. Burns?"

"I have. You employed me."

"And what did I employ you to do?"

He glanced at the judge, then back at me. "To remove the doorknob from the back door of Bob Shorter's house."

I pulled the doorknob and dead bolt from the box with the air of a magician pulling a rabbit out of the hat. There did seem to be a mild stirring of interest in the jury box.

"Can you tell us what these are?" I asked Rodney.

"They're the doorknob and dead bolt off Bob Shorter's back door."

"The defendant Robert Shorter?"

"Yes. It was his back door."

I carried doorknob and dead bolt to the prosecutor's table. "Would you like a closer look?"

Maxwell took first the dead bolt, then the doorknob from me and handed them back. I carried them to the judge. After I got the court clerk to put a number on each, I took the doorknob and dead bolt to Rodney Burns. "When did you get this doorknob and this dead bolt?" I asked him.

"Shortly after one o'clock this afternoon, maybe one fifteen or one twenty."

"Your Honor, I move to have the doorknob and dead bolt admitted into evidence."

Maxwell stood as Judge Cooley frowned, the judge's mouth puckering and his bushy white eyebrows coming together. "Objection," Maxwell said. "Relevance. This is another line of testimony that seems to have nothing to do with the issues at hand."

Judge Cooley nodded. "Perhaps you'd better make it clear to us how these items relate to the case."

I said, "As I indicated in my opening statement, it's the contention of the defense that Mr. Shorter has been framed, that some person or persons unknown entered into his house to take a paring knife from his kitchen and clothes from his closet and later reentered his house to plant the bloodstained clothes."

"Go on."

"That person or persons had to enter through the door of Mr. Shorter's house, a door locked by this door knob and this dead bolt."

"And the locks show signs of having been forced or picked? Mr. Burns is going to testify to that effect?"

"No, Your Honor. It is not my contention that the locks were picked. Recall that a house key was kept on a nail in the toolshed in the defendant's backyard."

"As I remember it, a witness testified only to looking for a key."

"And finding an empty nail," I said nodding.

"Ms. Steering. I'm afraid you're going to have to give us something more before we can admit those items into evidence."

I took a breath. "Very well." I turned back to the witness. "Mr. Burns, is the dead bolt currently locked or unlocked?"

He held it up. The thumb-turn was screwed into the housing, and the deadbolt itself stuck out through the strike plate. "I can't tell. I think it's unlocked."

It looked locked to me, but I retrieved Bill Hill's key ring from the court clerk and took it to Rodney. "Can you tell us what this is?"

"A key ring with four keys on it."

"This key ring has been admitted into evidence as the key ring that was found in the pants pocket of Bill Hill, the decedent in this case. Could you try the keys on the dead bolt to see if one of them will lock the dead bolt?"

He selected one of the keys and tried to insert it in the lock, but it didn't fit. My mouth had gone dry, and my heart had begun to hammer. I had staked my whole case and possibly my career on this moment, not to mention Bob Shorter's life.

Rodney tried another key. It went in.

And turned. The bolt clicked out another inch or so.

"Does that same key work the doorknob?"

Rodney wriggled the doorknob to show us that it wouldn't turn. He fitted the key to the lock and turned it. Unlocked, the doorknob turned freely.

"Your Honor," I said, looking up at the judge. "I renew my motion that the doorknob and dead bolt be admitted into evidence."

Maxwell stood. "These two items came off the back door of the defendant's house?" he asked Rodney.

"Yes, sir."

"Just today?"

"On the lunch break."

"And they are in the same condition as they were when you found them? They haven't been altered in any way?"

"Well, there's not a door connected to them anymore," Rodney said.

Maxwell ignored the titter that swept the courtroom. "You haven't rekeyed the locks," he said. "You have not altered the locking mechanism in any way."

"I have not."

Maxwell made a face. "No objection," he told the judge.

"Motion granted," the judge said. "The doorknob and dead bolt are admitted into evidence."

I said, "Those are all my questions of this witness."

"Mr. Maxim?"

"No further questions."

"Ms. Standing?" the judge said.

"The defense rests."

His eyebrows went up. "Very well. We'll go to closing arguments. Mr. Maximus?"

Chapter 19

Mr. Maximus, although he seemed a bit bewildered by the testimony of Dr. Gore and Rodney Burns, made a very coherent closing argument that reiterated his original theory of the case and referred neither to Bill Hill's medications nor to Bob Shorter's doorknob, at least not directly. He did warn the jury that an attempt had been made to introduce facts that had little or no bearing on the question of the defendant's guilt or innocence. "Focus your mind on the relevant facts," he told them. "The defendant had nothing but ill will for Bill Hill. On previous occasions he injured Mr. Hill's dog, and he left Mr. Hill himself by the side of the road in a snowstorm. The murder weapon in this case was the defendant's own knife, which bore his fingerprints and no one else's. None of these facts have been disputed. Despite the assertions of the defendant's lawyer to the contrary, the most likely explanation for the defendant's own blood-spattered clothes in the defendant's own closet is that the defendant himself left them there when he took them off after killing Bill Hill. That is the most reasonable, it is the only reasonable, interpretation of the facts of the case." Maxwell took a seat less than thirty minutes after he had begun his argument.

I went to the lectern. "Members of the jury. I have conceded that I have an unsympathetic client, but we are not here to determine whether or not Bob Shorter is a good man or a bad man. We are here to determine, if we can, whether it is beyond a reasonable doubt that Bob Shorter killed Bill Hill on March 9. The theory of the case I'm about to lay before you accounts for all of the evidence and accounts for it better than the theory you have just heard from the prosecution." I turned to give a nod to Ian Maxwell that he did not return.

"Bill Hill hated his neighbor Bob Shorter," I said, turning back to the jury, "and he had good reason to. Bob Shorter beat Mr. Hill's dog so badly that it eventually had to be put to sleep. His idea of a practical joke, driving off and leaving Mr. Hill in a snowstorm, cost him the front part of his foot. Day after day, Bob Shorter took his daily walks past Mr. Hill's residence, and Mr. Hill, who could walk only with increasing difficulty, could do no more than watch.

"Of course, Mr. Hill suffered from more than a partially missing foot. He had a progressive, disabling illness for which there is no cure. It was coming to the point that he was going to have to give up his home and move into an institution of some sort. Looking forward, he saw only increasing disability, increasing pain, and an unpleasant death. All this quite naturally had a depressing effect on his emotional well-being, and his treating physician has told you that he prescribed an antidepressant to combat it. Still, Bob Shorter persisted in walking past his house every day, walking with an easy gait and swinging the ax handle he called his equalizer, the picture of health.

"March 9 was the day Bill Hill could stand it no longer. When Bob Shorter left on one of his long walks, Mr. Hill made his way, with difficulty, to Shorter's house. Having once been close friends with the defendant, Mr. Hill knew where he kept his spare key. He got it from the toolshed and let himself into Shorter's house. It was a cold day, and Mr. Hill was wearing a jacket and gloves, all of which he was still wearing when his body was found. He would have left no fingerprints in Shorter's house.

"He took a paring knife from the counter in Shorter's kitchen—it was sheer luck that it had three of Shorter's fingerprints on it—and took it back into the closet in Shorter's bedroom. After finding a shirt and a pair of pants that Shorter had recently worn—maybe in a laundry hamper, on the end of the bed, draped over a clothes tree—he let down his own pants, cut his thigh with the paring knife, and bloodied Shorter's clothes. He closed the cut on his thigh with a butterfly bandage and tossed the bloody clothes back against the wall under Shorter's hanging clothes. When he pulled up his pants, he failed to notice that a small pillbox had fallen from his pocket. That pillbox contained Rilutek, a prescription medication for ALS, a condition that he had and the defendant Bob Shorter did not. Mr. Hill took the paring knife back to his own house with him. Probably, he would have liked to return the key to the shed in Shorter's backyard. Perhaps he simply didn't have the strength for it. Perhaps he didn't even notice the key until he had returned home, when there was nothing he could do but slide the key onto his own ring and hope it would not be noticed. He had one more task.

"If he wanted one final victory over the man who had done him so much harm, he not only had to kill himself, but had to do it with the paring knife he had taken from Bob Shorter's house. I can only imagine the despair and hatred that would have given him the strength to do it. He took the beechwood handle in his gloved hands, and he drove the blade into his chest. It may be hard for us to imagine a man doing such a thing, but remember, there were no defensive wounds on Mr. Hill's hands or forearms to indicate he had tried to ward off an attacker. There were no defensive wounds because Bill Hill was his own killer. He fell forward from his chair onto the floor and found, possibly to his surprise, that he was not yet dead. He touched his hand to his bleeding chest and used his blood-tipped finger to scrawl Shorter's name on the wood flooring. It was done. The frame was complete. About thirty minutes later, Bill Hill died from blood loss."

I stepped away from the lectern, wanting nothing between me and the jury as I made my final pitch. "Do we know with one hundred percent certainty that this was what happened? Probably not. Certainty is something usually denied to juries. Juries have to deal in probabilities. If you think there is a reasonable possibility that the sequence of events was something like the one I have just described, then it is your duty to find the defendant not guilty. And it is a reasonable possibility, one that explains facts that the prosecution's theory cannot explain: the key to Shorter's house in Bill Hill's pocket, the pillbox containing Bill Hill's medications on the floor of Shorter's closet, the wound on Bill Hill's thigh."

I swept my gaze over the faces of the jurors, meeting the eyes of all of them who would look at me. "The prosecution has itself presented evidence that Bill Hill had reason to hate Bob Shorter. That hatred provides a powerful motive for Mr. Hill's attempt to frame him for the crime of murder. I am sure you do not like Bob Shorter yourselves. He is not a likable man. But as much as you may shrink from doing it, your duty is to acquit if you have any reasonable doubt that he drove that knife into Bill Hill. Bob Shorter may have a lot to answer for, but punishment for those crimes must rest in the hands of a higher tribunal."

When I sat down, the energy seemed to drain from my body and puddle on the floor. I hardly heard Maxwell's rebuttal argument. When the judge gave his charge to the jury, I was vaguely glad to hear him emphasizing some of the points I had made regarding the prosecution's burden of proof and the presumption of innocence. He finished the charge, and the jury stood and exited the courtroom to begin their deliberations.

Shorter and I waited in one of the courthouse's smaller conference rooms.

"How long are we going to have to wait?" he asked.

"Don't know. Probably, the judge will give them until five thirty or six o'clock, then send them home for the night."

"They haven't been sequestered?"

I shook my head.

"So how do you think it's going to go?"

"I don't know. We're about to find out whether a group of trustworthy citizens is willing to let an open sociopath go free."

"I'm not a sociopath."

"No? Don't you reject any moral or legal claims on your behavior?"

"Not at all. I obey the law. I have to as a matter of self-preservation."

"But you don't have a conscience."

"Let's just say I don't let it bother me."

"And you have no regard for the rights of others."

"What rights? If you mean extralegal rights, then no. It's nonsense to talk about people having rights other than those the law gives them."

"And you show a proclivity for violence, at least toward dogs. I think we're getting pretty close to the definition of a sociopath."

"Morality is all about power, you know. Of course, the law is, too—it's just that the law is more obviously about power. The majority of our fellow citizens are a bunch of sheep, and they pass laws in an effort to control the wolves in their midst. They push their moral conventions the same way: they ostracize people and apply social pressure where they can't enact legal penalties."

"So you think morality is all a matter of self-interest," I said.

"Exactly."

"For you, morality isn't even the majority opinion about right and wrong," I said.

"There is no such thing as right and wrong."

I didn't know how to refute that statement with logical argument. I did have an impulse to leap on Shorter and choke the life out of him, but I resisted it.

Shorter said, "What are you thinking?"

"I'm wondering what the difference is between a sociopath and a psychopath."

His eyes cut to the ceiling. "More labels. I'm a realist, that's all."

I presented my last argument, reluctantly because I wasn't sure that it would stand up to Shorter's assault. "What about God?" I said.

"What about heaven and Jesus and the saints and the prophets?" He blew a raspberry.

"You think it's all superstition?"

"Oh, come on. Is that the basis of your morality? 'I can't do this, I can't do that, because God wouldn't like it'?"

"I prefer to think of it as living my life in conformity to the character of God, doing what pleases him."

"And who told you there was a God? Your mommy and your daddy? Can't you see it was an effort to control your behavior from the cradle? I don't blame them, you understand. By that time, your parents themselves had experienced a lifetime of conditioning."

"I don't accept that."

"Do you go to church?"

I moved my head equivocally.

"So you don't believe, not really—and you can't. You're too smart for that."

"I believe in God or whatever or whoever gives us a moral sense, a sense that some things are inherently right and some things are inherently wrong. I believe in a moral awareness that makes us human." It felt a little like the recitation of a creed.

Shorter studied me, and I met his gaze, not blinking even as my eyes began to water.

There was a tap on the door, and a woman put her head in. "The jury's reached a verdict," she said.

A few more seconds passed, then Shorter broke eye contact and stood. "That was fast," he said.

"Very fast," I agreed.

"I'm thinking that can't be good."

"We'll see."

The jury filed into the courtroom. They sat. The bailiff called the court to order, and the judge swept in. "Has the jury reached its verdict?" he asked.

Andrew Hartman stood, the young man with the sense of humor, the foreman I would have picked if the choice had been up to me rather than his fellow jurors. "We have, Your Honor," he said. He gave a form to the bailiff, who took it to the judge. The judge read it, nodded, and gave it back to the bailiff.

"Stand for the reading of the verdict."

We stood, the members of the jury and all of us before the bar—Shorter and me and Ian Maxwell. The bailiff read from the form, "We, the members of the jury, find the defendant, Robert Shorter, not guilty of the crime of murder in the first degree."

There was no reaction from the gallery behind us. I exhaled and glanced at Shorter, who looked back at me without smiling.

Judge Cooley said, "Robert Shorter, you have been tried by a jury of your peers and found not guilty. Members of the jury, I thank you for your service. This court is adjourned."

The reaction from the gallery began as the murmur of voices from a dozen conversations, then two dozen, then three. As the volume grew, the judge exited the courtroom. Shorter held out his hand. I looked at it and then took it. "You're a confused young woman, but I wasn't wrong about you," he said. "You know your stuff."

My mouth stretched. "Justice, no matter who it's for or against," I said. I'd finally gotten around to looking up the phrase on the Internet. It was a quote from Malcolm X. I had no idea how it had gotten stuck in my brain.

The corner of Shorter's mouth rose, revealing once again those yellow teeth. "How long will it take me to get my doorknob back?" he asked.

"I don't know. A while."

"Well, I won't wait for it." He gave me a curt nod and went around me to push his way through the bar. The spectators moved and shuffled to make way for him as he walked down the aisle. He passed through the open door and was gone.

My gaze went to my friends, then to Rodney Burns and Dr. Gore beside him. I got nods, a smile or two, and a thumbs-up from Paul. I smiled. When I glanced toward the jury box, one of the jurors was waving me over. A big woman in her fifties, she reached across the rail to put a meaty hand on my arm.

"You're too nice a young lady to be associated with that awful man," she said.

I gave her a lopsided smile. "Thank you. My association seems to be over now."

"Even if we couldn't convict him for this—and we couldn't, we all knew we couldn't—he ought to go to prison for what he did to Mr. Hill, leaving him in a snowstorm that way just for his own amusement. And what he did to that dog! I have two little Pomeranians myself, and I'd give him the electric chair just for that. I'd be willing to throw the switch myself."

"Me, too," I told her. "I have a Lab."

Andrew Hartman was just leaving the courtroom; he turned back in the doorway and caught me looking at him. He gave me a nod and a mocking smile, and then he was gone.

Shorter's neighbors were waiting for me outside the courthouse doors—Jenn, Valerie, Mark Rehrer, and several I didn't even know.

"So you did it, didn't you?" Jenn said. "You managed to smear my son and get that murdering devil off."

I had my own coterie of supporters, Paul and Brooke and Mike. Paul stepped in front of me, but I put a hand to his shoulder and urged him to one side.

"I didn't see you in the courtroom," I said. "Any of you."

"We know what happened," Valerie said.

"I think your son was in my neighborhood last night," I told Jenn. "Larkin and his buddies and a handful of firecrackers."

"Larkin was home watching TV."

I nodded. "Better keep him there."

"What do you mean by that? Is that a threat?"

Valerie said, "I know there's not much we can do to you. File a complaint with the state bar association, maybe."

"Larkin's done it already. We'll see how far it goes."

Jenn's expression was as close to a snarl as anything I'd seen on a human face.

"How did you get to Melissa?" Mark asked. "We know about her part in this."

"I served her with a subpoena, threatened her with contempt of court if she didn't show." I smiled. "She didn't have a lot of choice in the matter."

"You are a hateful, hateful woman," Valerie said.

I nodded. "I'm a hateful woman who believes a man should be held accountable for the crimes he has committed and not those he hasn't."

"What do you mean by that?" Mark said.

"Wait and see."

Chapter 20

I met Hernandez and Jordan in a bar on Strawberry Street in Richmond's Fan district. They already had their beers and were halfway through an order of potato skins when I sat down.

Hernandez signaled the waiter. "Get this woman a drink," he said. "She's earned it."

"A glass of Riesling," I told the waiter. To Hernandez I said, "Earned it? By helping a bad man go free?"

"Not for that. For what you did afterward."

"Shorter's back in jail," Jordan said. "With Melissa Stimmler's testimony and that video evidence of hers—"

Hernandez said, "We've got the testimony of Mark Rehrer, too, the guy who lives across from Bill Hill and Melissa. Turns out he remembers seeing that shepherd dog after Shorter finished beating it to death. He thought at first it had been hit by a car, until we showed him Melissa's video."

"After Shorter got no more than a fine for what he did to Bill Hill's dog, Melissa didn't think it would do much good to report him," I said. "And of course she was scared of him. Still is, no doubt, but she's been in the witness stand now and discovered that testifying is something she can do."

My wine came, and I took a sip. It had a crisp, fruity flavor. I thought Riesling might be my new favorite for the coming summer.

"Have a potato skin," Hernandez said. "They're still warm."

"I'm meeting someone for dinner."

"A fine is still a conviction," Jordan said. "It's that prior conviction that gives these new charges such punch," Jordan said.

I nodded and sipped my wine. In Virginia, a second conviction for cruelty to animals was a class-six felony.

"One to five years," Hernandez said, pushing most of a potato skin into his mouth. He nodded with apparent satisfaction as he chewed.

"One thing we wanted to ask you," Jordan said, "the reason we asked you to meet us here."

"The reason we bought you a drink," Hernandez said.

"You're not going to represent Shorter on this, are you?"

I smiled and shook my head.

"Suppose he offers you a big pile of money," Hernandez suggested.

"I have a dog whom I love dearly. There isn't enough money."

"So you'll represent him when he's accused of killing a human being, just not when he's accused of something really bad like killing a dog."

"I didn't know he was guilty of killing the human being. I do know he beat the dog to death."

"Isn't he entitled to his day in court?" Jordan asked.

I nodded. "Sure he is, just not with me sitting next to him."

"I never thought I'd say this to a lawyer," Hernandez said, "but you've got integrity."

"Don't let it get around. We've got a reputation to maintain.